MIYAMOTO MUSASHI
TWO SWORDS

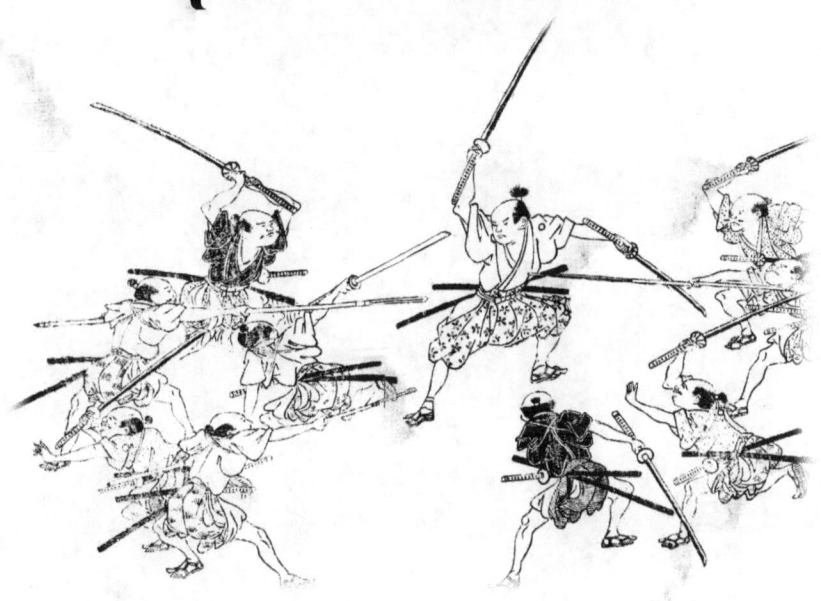

An Illustrated Tale of Bravery
Book 2 (Volumes 3 & 4 of 10)
Published 1803

Written by Hiraga Baisetsu
Illustrated by Hayami Shungyosai
Translated by Eric Shahan

巖流敵討繪本二島英勇記
Revenge Killing of Ganryu: Two Islands (Swords)
An Illustrated Tale of Bravery
Volume III

Written by Hiraga Baisetsu 平賀梅雪
Illustrated by Hayami Shungyosai 速水春暁斎
Published 1803

Book 3
Table of Contents

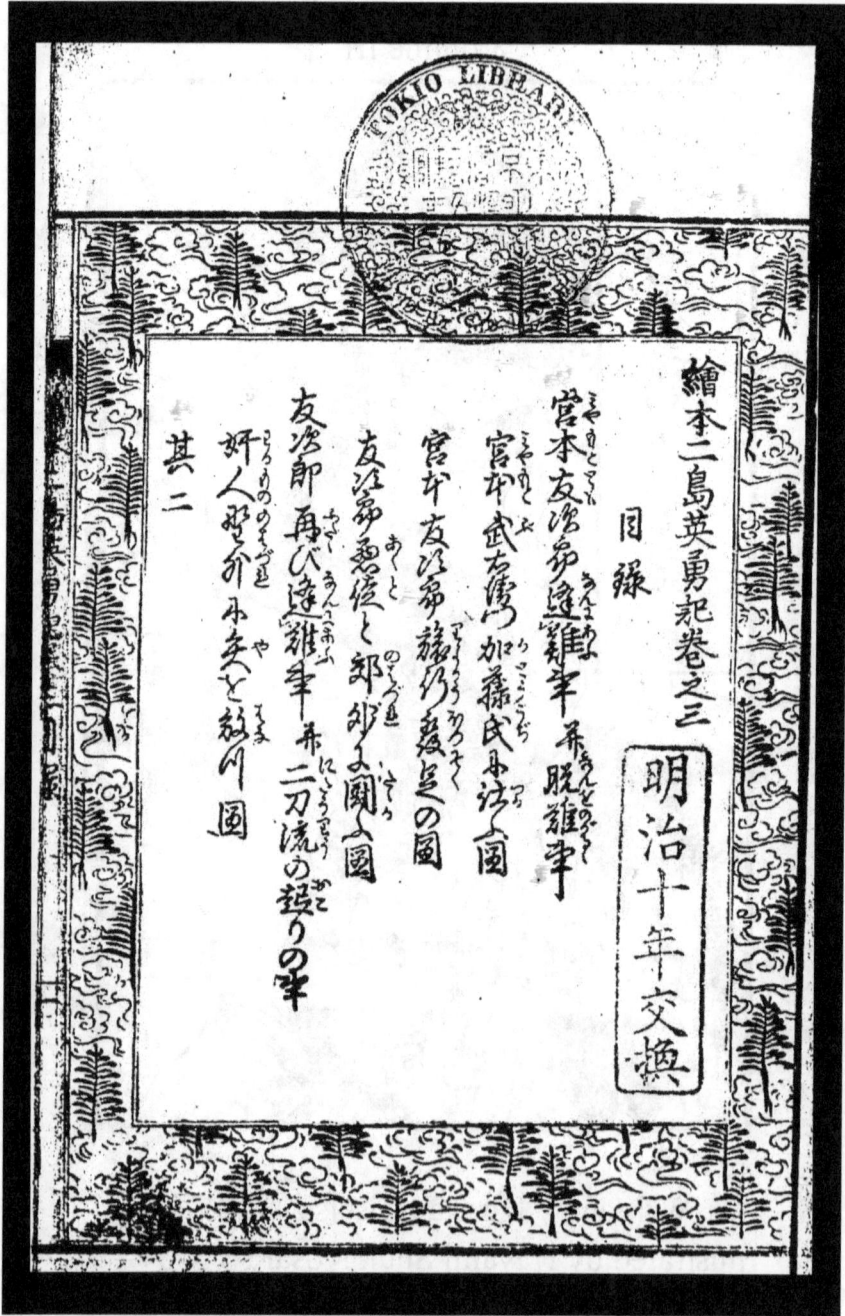

繪本二島英勇記
Two Swords
An Illustrated Tale of Bravery

卷之三　目録
Book Three　Table of Contents

Book 3
Table of Contents

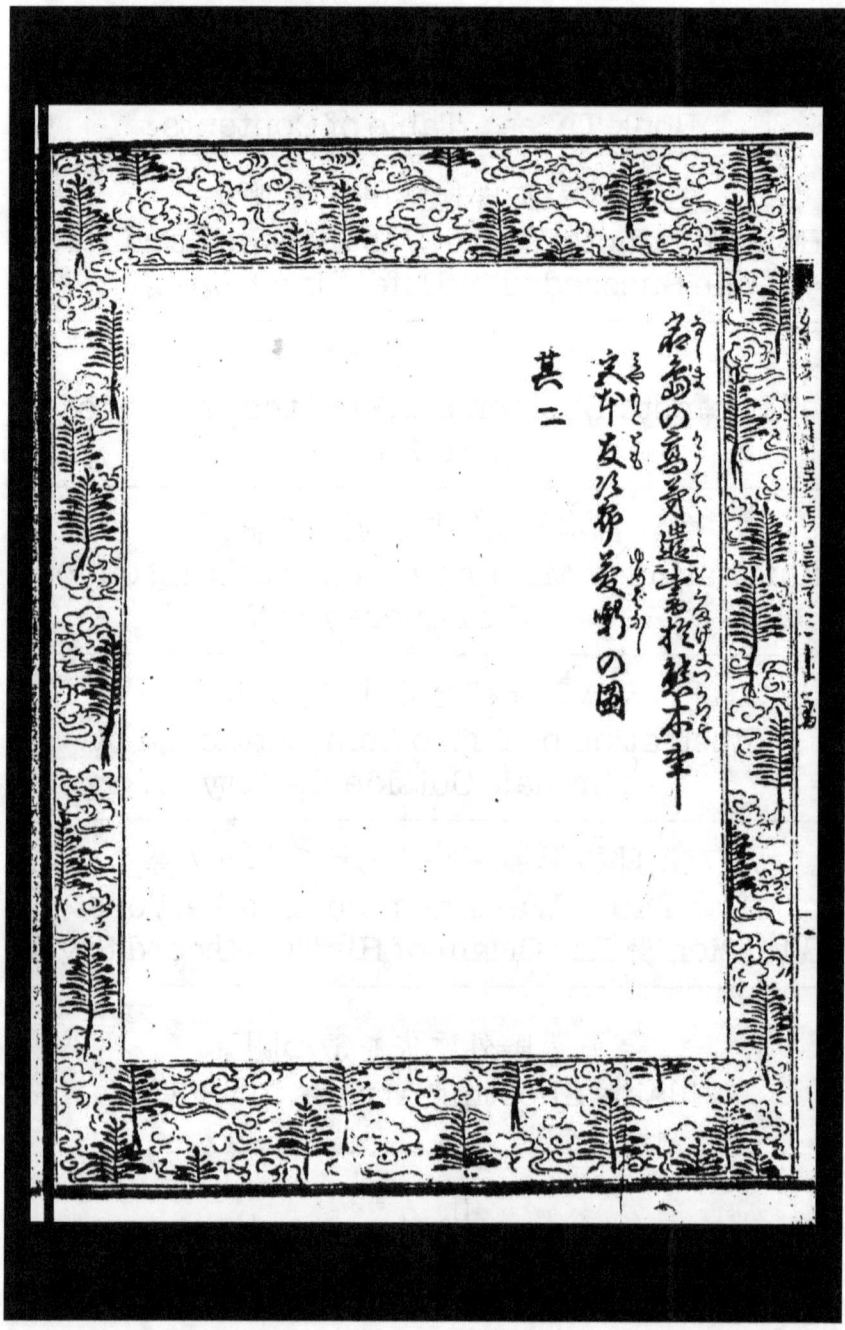

繪本二島英勇記
Two Swords
An Illustrated Tale of Bravery

卷之三　目録
Book Three　Table of Contents

FEUDAL MAP OF JAPAN
BETWEEN 1564–73
Provinces in Capital letters
Daimyo in Italics
Smaller Daimyo

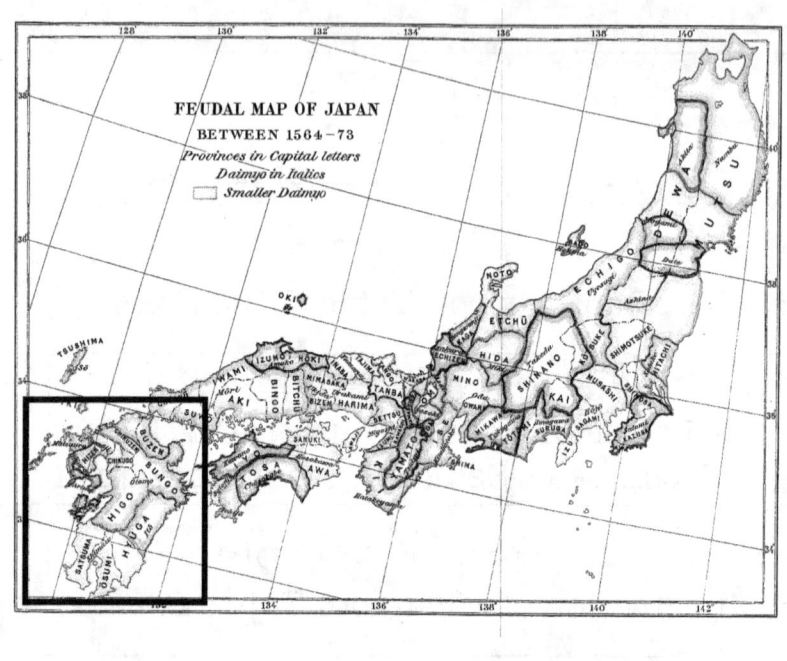

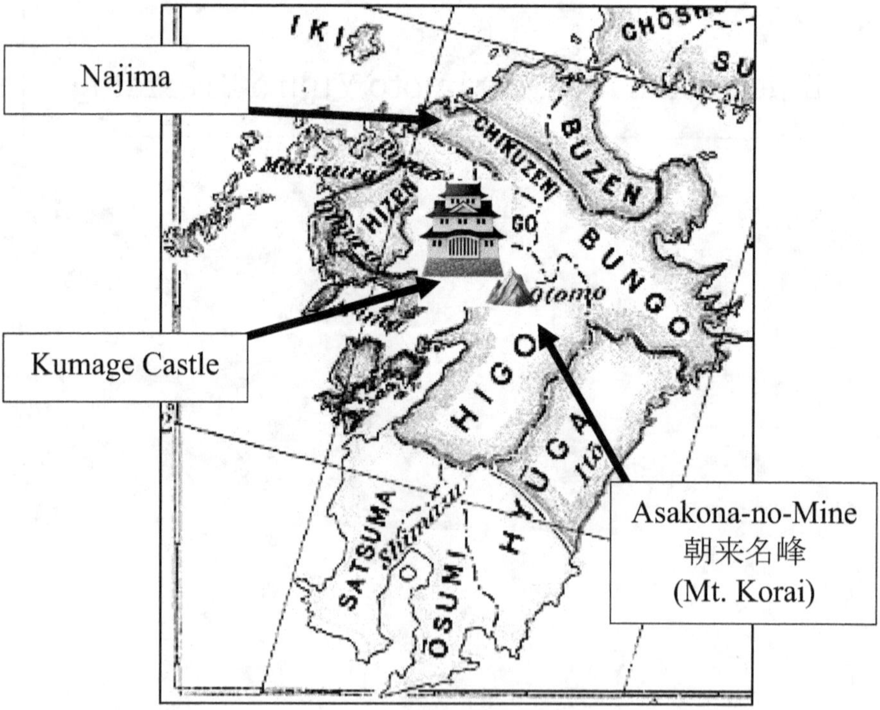

Najima
Kumage Castle
Asakona-no-Mine
朝来名峰
(Mt. Korai)
IKI
CHIKUZEN
BUZEN
BUNGO
HIZEN
Matsuura
Otomo
HIGO
HYUGA
SATSUMA
ŌSUMI
Shimazu

宮本友次郎逢難事并脱難事
How Miyamoto Yujiro Was Attacked and How He Succeeded in Defending Himself

The book *Record of Higo Domain: Customs and Traditions* is a Fudoki. Fudoki were reports on the history, geography, myths and folklore of a region which were presented to the Emperor of Japan. By reading Fudoki, the Emperor could learn about local areas.

The *Record of Higo Domain* states that long ago, in the rein of Emperor Sujin (148 ~ 30 BC,) there was a group of renegades called Tsuchi-gumo, Dirt Spiders, who did not accept Emperor Sujin and his Yamato Court as their ruler. Around 180 of these Dirt Spiders lived on the peak of Mt. Asakona-no-Mine 朝来名峰, present day Mt. Asako 朝来山 in Kyushu. The leaders of the Dirt Spiders were named Striking Monkey and Head Monkey. They hid out on the peak of the mountain and ignored the orders of their rightful ruler. Emperor Sujin commanded one of his commanders, Takeokumi, who later founded Hikimi Domain, to destroy the criminals.

Takeokumi immediately set to work ridding the world of the Dirt Spiders. Having finished his task, Takeokumi started home. Since the sun was beginning to set he decided to spend the night on White Hair Mountain in the Yatsushiro region. Suddenly, out of nowhere, the night sky behind the mountains was lit up by fire. The fire, which had started naturally, soon spread across the whole range of mountains. Takeokumi was astounded, and later, when he had an audience with the emperor, he reported the strange event. The emperor responded to the story with an imperial decree that the region be called Hi-no-Kuni, giving the area Kanji that meant "Domain of Fire 火の国." Later generations would change the initial Kanji from "Fire 火" to one meaning "Fertile 肥," albeit with the same reading.

Later, this domain was divided two, and that is why we have Hizen 備前 "Fertile Former" and Higo 肥後 "Fertile Latter." Bigo Domain covers the south-western area, and is surrounded by mountains and the sea. The area receives lots of sunshine and even in the cooler months the area stays warm. It is a farming domain and it produces far and away the largest rice crop in the whole country. This excellent domain contains vast swaths of fertile land.

Translator's Notes:

Fudoki are thought to have originated in the early 8th century. The *Continuation of the Chronicles of* Japan 続日本紀 notes five categories were to be reported in Fudoki:

1) Write the names of the districts and villages in the various provinces in the capital area and the seven circuits with two auspicious Kanji

2) Report on the various kinds of minerals, animals, and vegetation found in each district

3) Record the fertility of the land

4) Record the origins of the names of mountains, rivers, plains, and moors

5) Record old stories and strange events as remembered by the elderly in the area, and report these as historical accounts

Tsuchigumo 土蜘蛛"dirt/earth spider"

Tsuchigumo is a historical Japanese derogatory term for renegade local clans, and also the name for a race of spider-like Yokai, or supernatural creatures, in Japanese folklore. In art, they are depicted as ferocious supernatural beasts. Illustration below from *Tsuchigumo Illustrated Scroll* 土蜘蛛草紙絵巻 Edo Era.

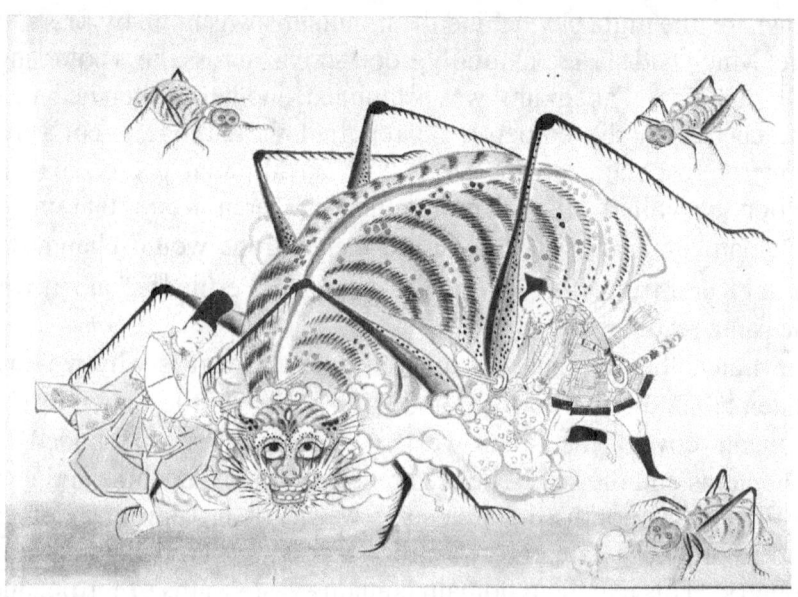

Dirt Spider Scroll 土蜘蛛草紙 Early Edo Era
This scroll shows a more humanoid Dirt Spider who was
terrorizing locals until they decapitated him.

While Dirt Spiders continued to appear as adversaries into the Heian Era. In the illustration below titled *The Illustrated Life of Yoirmitsu* 頼光一代記圖繪 (1858) depicts Minamoto no Yorimitsu 源頼光 (948 ～ 1021) killing a troublesome Dirt Spider.

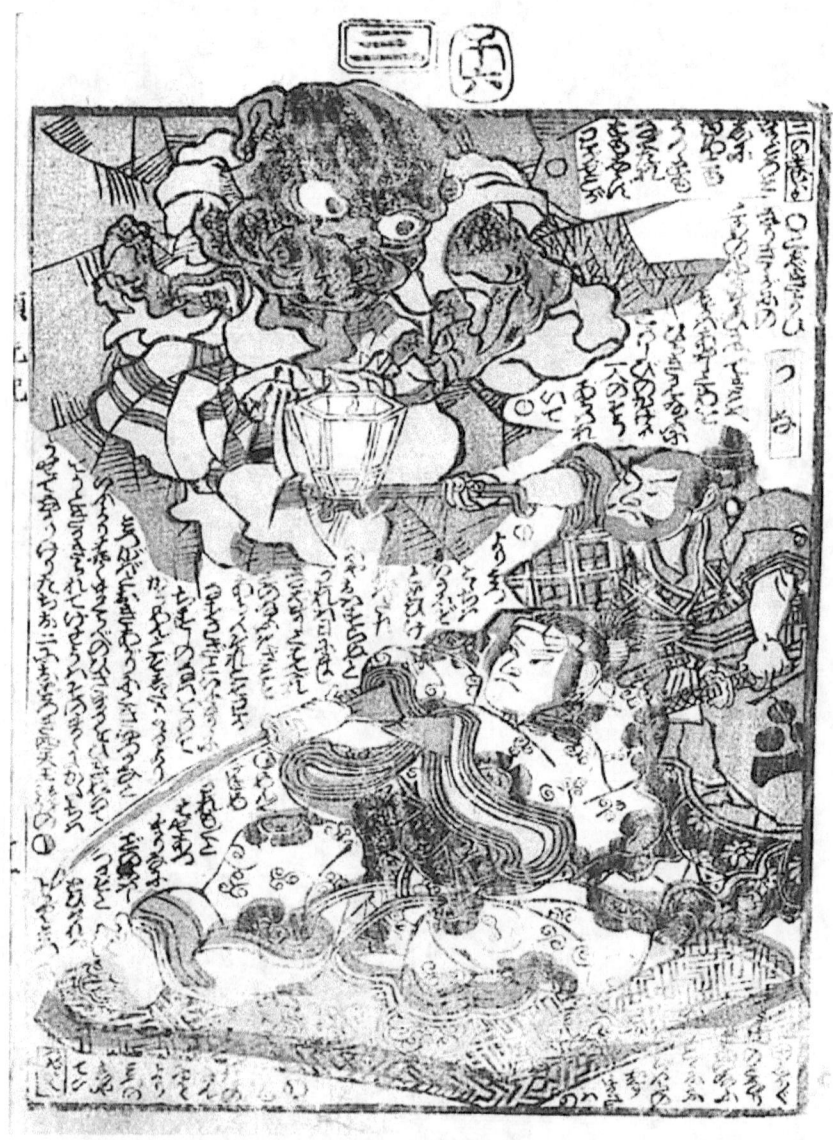

End Translator's Notes

So, returning to the story, at this time Kumage Castle[1] was under the control of Sato Kiyomasa, Head of the Budget, for the imperial court. He was a ruler who was adept at both written learning and martial arts. Further, since Kiyomasa always stressed the importance of filial piety, the common folk absorbed these lessons and used them to guide their daily lives. Thus, families in this region were prosperous and sang songs of peace.

Kumage Domain is located at the westernmost end of Japan, therefore it is the part of Japan closest to foreign countries. Due to this proximity, Lord Sato Kiyomasa was strict about military preparedness. The Samurai who served him trained extensively in horseback archery and their sword technique was said to be the best in the country. If anyone from this region accepted an invitation to train in another school of martial arts, they invariably excelled.

Lord Kiyomasa knew of Miyamoto Buemon before he was granted control of Kumage Castle. Miyamoto Buemon had discovered the inner mysteries of all six of the major martial arts: bow, horse, sword, spear, matchlock and jujutsu. He was originally from the Uchi Region of Yamashiro Domain and had devoted his life to the study of martial arts. Later, he met Yoshioka Taro Uemon and became an devoted to his martial arts method. Miyamoto Buemon trained day and night without fail and after about three years the difference in skill between Buemon and his master Yoshioka Taro Uemon all but disappeared. Taro Uemon was mightily impressed by this and decided to reveal the inner secrets of his art to Miyamoto Buemon. Thus, Buemon received the Okumyo, transmission of the inner mysteries of the art.

Lord Kiyomasa, the head of the imperial accounting bureau, having heard about Miyamoto Buemon's famous ability in martial arts, invited him enter his service. Buemon agreed to become a retainer of Lord Kiyomasa, and he traveled to Najima in Tsukuzen in order to inform his teacher Yoshioka.

---

[1] The author changed the name of the domain and castle from Kuma*moto* to Kuma*ge* and the name of the lord from *Kato* Kiyomasa to *Sato* Kiyomasa. This was to make the book "a work of fiction" and not a historical tale.

宮本武右衛門加藤氏に仕ふ圖
Miyamoto Buemon entering the employ of Lord Kato
(The rest of the story lists him as Lord *Sato*)

Miyamoto Buemon said, "It is with profound hesitation I would like to announce that I have become a retainer for the bravest warrior in Japan, Lord Sato Kiyomasa. I plan to follow this great man and use his example to increase my own prestige. However, as you know, I am without a son. Sensei, you have been fortunate enough to have been blessed with two sons. I would like to request that you permit me to adopt your second son, Yujiro, and allow me to raise him with love. I will teach him all the inner secrets of the sword that you have taught to me. By teaching young lord Yujiro all the lessons you taught me, without exception, it will allow my teacher's sword art and philosophy of training to spread to every corner of Japan. Sensei, what do you think of my plan?"

Yoshioka was delighted and said warmly, "To tell you the truth this is exactly what I wanted. Please adopt and raise Yujiro. However, he is still in diapers, so I can't be sure if there will be any difficulties raising him. If, after he is grown, he ends up being worthless do not waste your time with pity, but expel him from your house. Should that situation arise, understand it will not cause me to hold a grudge."

"Further, if in the future a child and heir is born to you, that child would be linked to you by blood. Thus, that child would be your true successor. If that occurs send Yujiro back to me. A person with a direct blood link to you should be your successor, this is the best way to honor your ancestors. Do not feel any hesitation regarding this."

Buemon was profoundly honored by his teacher's words and, taking the two-year-old Yujiro in his arms and holding him to his chest, he returned with his adopted child to serve Lord Kiyomasa.

So, Buemon loved and cared for his adopted child Yujiro. He paid attention to his development and saw that he trained diligently in martial arts day and night without fail. Yujiro was naturally a brave and dedicated boy and by the time he was 12 or 13 years old he had naturally developed a nimble style, that was unmatched even by long time disciples of Buemon, who had trained for many years. Buemon dearly loved Yujiro and instructed him in the inner mysteries of his sword art.

When Yujiro turned 14, Buemon and his wife had a son. They named him Yunosuke. However, though Yunosuke was directly related to him, Buemon did not think of Yunosuke as his successor.

On the contrary, Miyamoto Buemon grew more attached to Yujiro, his adopted son. Buemon's dedicated even more of his mental energy to Yujiro's instruction. Yujiro, for his part, revered his adoptive father. When Yujiro turned 15 he received complete transmission in every secret of his father's art. In addition, Miyamoto Yujiro had a good reputation in Lord Kiyomasa's household. Many thought Yujiro's skill exceeded that of his father and they lionized him as the reincarnation of a Tengu, a mountain goblin who teaches martial arts.

However, as the saying goes, *The wind hates tall trees*, soon other martial artists, who were full of pride, gathered together and began to spread rumors about Yujiro. Other schools took a particular dislike to him. They got together and said things like, "If we ever get the chance, I think we need to surprise Yujiro and strike a little fear into him. That will take him down a peg or two."

As it turned out, that chance never came because in March of the 16th year of Tensho (1588,) Sato Kiyomasa, the head of the imperial accounting bureau, was granted control of Kumage Castle in Higo Domain. Thus, when Yujiro turned 17, the Miyamoto family moved to Higo domain.

That year in August, when autumn was just beginning, Yujiro stood before his father and said, "I have a request, Mt. Aso lies in this domain and it is truly one of the most spiritual mountains in all of Japan. It is said to be the foremost of the five great mountains of our imperial land. Thus I would very much like to go there and climb Mt. Aso and experience the area myself. If you were to grant me 6 or 7 days of leave, I would like to travel there and, after climbing, visit some of the famous spots in that area."

In response to this request Buemon, nodded and said, "That sounds like a fine plan to me, I approve. Since you will only be gone six or seven days there is no need to confirm this with Lord Sato. Go and do as you please."

Mountains of Higo Domain 五ヶの庄 1856
By Utagawa Hiroshige (1797–1858)

宮本友次郎旅行發足の圖
Illustration of Miyamoto Yujiro Setting out on His Journey

Yujiro immediately began his travel preparations. He intended to leave before dawn on the morning of August 18th, and travel alone without a servant. Therefore, on the night of the 17th he prepared all his gear and laid it above his pillow. That night he went to bed early.

Somehow word of Yujiro's trip reached the ears of the jealous Samurai. They were a proud bunch, always strutting about and five or six of them whispered to each other, "This is a great opportunity! If we wait just on the outskirts of the town around the base of the castle we can catch him by surprise, we'll leave him half dead and half alive."

Four of them decided to participate. Kondo Nabematsu studied spear fighting, Kumasawa Jinnojo studied the sword and Yamauchi Kanimaru and Oun Shinnosuke studied Jujutsu. All four had trained extensively in their art, were fearless and would take on any opponent. That night they searched for an appropriate spot to ambush Yujiro. Having located one, they went home.

So, on the morning of the 18th Yujiro woke, dressed for travel and readied his things. He set out at first light, just as the cocks were crowing. His few items of extra clothing were wrapped in a cloth and thrown over his shoulder and before long he was on the outskirts of the town below Kumage Castle. He walked in the direction of the rising sun, away from the moon, which was setting in the west.

He passed through an isolated village and a lonely guard dog barked at him. The droplets of dew in the fields sparked as they always did this time of year, though it seemed somewhat dreary this season. This was probably due to the wind blowing across the tops of the silvergrass, causing the rippling grass to seem like a morning storm.

Then, from somewhere, the high sound of someone whistling echoed across the field. Suddenly, both in front of him and behind, black clad figures emerged. There were four of them, all with their faces completely concealed. The figures attacked simultaneously, shouting as they moved in. One stabbed with a spear and the other three cut with Katana.

Yujiro remained unperturbed and dodged the attacks coming from both sides. One man cut down with his Katana aiming for Yujiro's head. He dropped down under this attack, fast as lightning.

Drawing his sword in a quick motion, Yujiro struck the attacker in front of him on his shoulder with Mine-uchi, a hit using the back of the blade.   The blow likely broke the man's collarbone and the black-clad figure collapsed to the ground without even a grunt of pain.

In fact, the man who crumpled on the ground was Taiun Shinnosuke. From the left and right Kumasawa Jinnojo and Yamauchi Kanimaru attacked simultaneously.   Yujiro spun around just in time to knock Kumazawa's Katana to the ground then Yujiro immediately leapt in and struck Kanimaru in Indo, the spot between his eyebrows.   This blow was also done with the back of his sword. Kanimaru was now out of the fight.

> Note:
> The striking point Indo 印堂 is another word for Miken 眉間, the spot between the eyebrows.

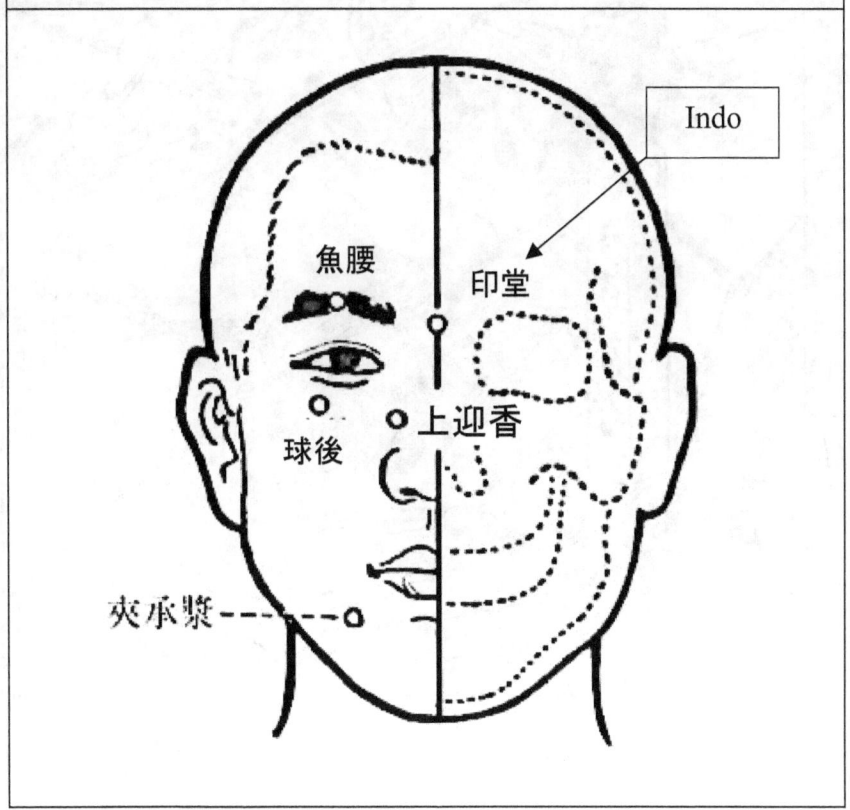

友次郎惡徒と郊外に闘ふ圖

Illustration of Yujiro Being Attacked By Criminals Outside the City

Kondo Nabematsu, realizing he had an while Yujiro was engaged with Kanimaru, stabbed forward with his spear, twisting it as he thrust. Yujiro, using a rapid Irimi, entering technique, ducked under the spearpoint and advanced, as fast as the sparkle of moonlight off a pool of water under a mountainside. He slipped past the spearpoint to where Kondo's hands were holding the shaft. As before, Yujiro did not strike with the blade but used the flat of his sword to hit Shin-eh, the top of the head. Kondo fell to the ground seeing stars.

Seeing the intensity of Yujiro's swordsmanship, Kumasawa Jinnojo realized the ambush was not going to succeed. So, without even bothering to recover his Katana, he turned and started to flee. Seeing this unbelievable act, Yujiro shouted, "You dishonorable thief! You see your brethren knocked down and you run away?! The actions of a coward!"

Catching up to him Yujiro struck him with a Mine-uchi, a hit with the back of his Katana, and Kumasawa collapsed to the ground unconscious.

Yujiro returned to where he was first attacked and found the men he struck curled up on the ground. They were showing signs of life, but remained unable to move their arms, much less rise after having been struck. Yujiro spoke and his angry voice was like thunder, "You all are nothing more than a bunch of bandits, that much is clear. The lord of this domain has infused this area with his honorable governance, thus the people of Bigo Domain do not even have to bar their doors at night. Is this not because everyone respects Lord Kiyomasa's rule? So, the fact that you men decided to cause a disturbance near Kumage Castle only compounds your crime and has left me speechless. It would have been a simple thing for me to cut you all down, however if I were to spill the blood of men like you with my two swords in order to quell a disturbance under the heavens, it would only serve to sully my blades. I think I will just stomp each of you to death. When you meet Enma, the lord of hell, and he is set to judge you, tell him that it was the foot of Miyamoto Yujiro that led you to this place. That way you can refuse his offer and go somewhere else."

Saying that he raised his foot to crush Kanimaru's windpipe. In a pained voice Kanimaru cried out, "Lord Yujiro, please forgive our crime and our insulting behavior. We are actually Samurai under the same lord. Frankly, we are astounded at your skill. When we attacked you, we did not do so as thieves, but as men doing Musha Shugyo to develop our martial arts skill. So, our attack was not to rob you but Ude-dameshi[2], to test our skill and strength with martial arts against a superior opponent. We were hanging around this area when we happened to catch sight of you. Since your skill with the sword is well known, we recognized you. We sought to test our skill against your famous sword art and gain some measure of fame for ourselves."

He continued, "We now understand attacking you was inglorious, and we have caused an unforgivable insult. We all humbly ask your forgiveness. If you are willing to accept our humble apology, then you will have our great thanks for your fantastic show of humanity."

The other three men, responding with noses pinched or with otherwise changed voices, said in unison, "It is just as that man said, please grant us the smallest sliver of your compassion!"

Yujiro immediately relaxed the foot he had been pressing into Kanimaru's neck and helped him up. He then helped all of the other men up. While he was doing this Yujiro said, "I completely understand your reasons. If indeed this battle was an Ude-dameshi, test of skill, as part of your training, then this fight cannot be described as a thoughtless indiscretion. In the end, both you and I are following the way of the sword. It occurs to me, if you are dedicated to training you would want to test out your techniques, in order to perfect your skills. Therefore, I see why doing Ude-dameshi is essential though I have not done such a thing myself. Perhaps I too need to apologize and ask your forgiveness for misunderstanding. Please do not harbor any grudge against me."

The three men answered in unison, "What reason would we have for holding a grudge? In truth we should remove our masks and apologize to your face for our crimes, however we, like you, have lost honor so please understand why we remain masked."

While doing this they bowed their heads and rubbed their hands together, feigning submissiveness.

---

[2] Note: Embarking on Musha Shugyo means traveling to other domains to train at the local Dojo. They would also engage in duels.

友次郎再逢難事并二刀流の起りの事
How Yujiro Was Again Put in a Perilous Situation & The Origin of His Nito Ryu, Two-Sword Style

So, with the matter settled, Yujiro not dwell on the dangerous situation he had just escaped from. He walked away from the Samurai who had ambushed him and hurriedly resumed his journey to Mount Aso.

According to *The Chronicles of Japan,* the first mention of the Aso Region of Higo Domain occurred during the reign of the 12th Emperor of Japan, Emperor Keiko (13 BC ~ 130 AD) who lived to be 143 years old. In the 18th year of his rein, around 89 AD, he set out for Tsukushi Domain for a hunting trip.

The Chronicles of Japan[3] (Completed in 720 AD)
Chapter 7: Emperor Keiko

May 1st 89 AD.
Setting sail from Ashikita, the Emperor proceeded to Hi-no-Kuni. Here the sun went down, and the night being dark, they did not know how to reach the shore. A fire was seen shining afar off, and the Emperor commanded the helmsman, saying, "Make straight for the place where the fire is." So he proceeded towards the fire, and thus was enabled to reach the shore. The Emperor made inquiry respecting the place where the fire was, saying, "What is the name of this village?" The people of the land answered and said, "Toyomura, in the district of Yatsushiro." Again, he made inquiry respecting the fire, "Whose fire is this?" But no owner could be found, and thereupon it was known that it was not a fire made by man. Therefore, that country was called Hi no Kuni, Fire Domain.

June 3rd 89 AD.

---

[3] This section is adapted from the translation by William G. Aston (1841 ~ 1911) first published in <u>Proceedings of Japan Society</u> in 1896.

The Emperor crossed over from the district of Takaku to the village of Tamakina. There was a thieving Tsuchi-gumo, Dirt Spider, that lived there but the Emperor destroyed it.

Emperor Keiko then went to the land of Aso. Since this happened long ago the area was still undeveloped. *The Chronicles of Japan* contains a description of this domain:

June 16th 89 AD.

The Emperor arrived at the Land of Aso. The land was wide and covered over with vegetation as far as the Emperor could see however there was no sign of human habitation. The Emperor said aloud, "Are there any people in this country? Or does no one live here?" Now there were two gods that lived there, a male God called Aso-tsu-hiko, a female God named Aso-tsu-hime. Upon hearing the Emperor speak they suddenly assuming human form, sauntered forward and said, "We two are here. How can it be said that there are no people?"

Hearing this the Emperor replied, "Then let this land be known as The Land of the Aso People.

A note on the word Aso, written 阿蘇 in Kanji. These days the word "Aso" can mean "you all over there" or "you folks." All the old language used in ancient times has fallen out of use these days, however a few words can still be found as names of places.

In olden times, when the emperor would command the retainers seated to his left and right he would say, "Aso, do this," or "Aso, do that." Even now in the imperial palace the courtiers are called Ason 朝臣. This name is a derivative of the word Aso that has been passed down from ancient times.[4]

Returning to the story, the two gods Aso Tsuhiko and Aso Tsuhime took up residence on Mount Aso and two shrines can be found dedicated to them. These are Takeiwatatsu no Mikoto Shrine and Aso Hime Kami Shrine. Both of these shrines are mentioned in the *Proceedings of the Engi Era* a 927 AD book that contains a discussion of laws and customs.

---

[4] This is the author speculating on linguistics

Yujiro climbed Mt. Aso by himself and, upon reaching the summit saw the amazing view in all directions. So impressed was he with the scenery that he found himself at a loss for words. The mountain is described in the *Customs and Geography of Tsukushi*. While the book *Customs and Geography of Tsukushi* has been lost, passages have been preserved in the *Annotated Chronicles of Japan,* an edition of *The Chronicles of Japan* with notations written by Urabe Kanekata sometime between 1274 and 1301.

Mt. Aso was described in chapter 10 of *Customs and Geography of Tsukushi* :

About 20 Ri south-west of Aso Prefecture in Higo Domain there is a tall mountain known as Aso ga Gaku. At the top of the mountain there is a lake of mysterious spiritual power. There are large stones that form a wall around the area and it is 150 meters long and 300 meters wide and over 60 meters deep. It is said the water is so clear that it makes it seem like the bottom, a hundred fathoms down, is lined with silver. This is hardly an exaggeration. The grand, tall shape of this steep mountain is spectacular to be hold. The shape seems to suggest it is ready to leap up and fly into the blue sky.

Yujiro spend the whole day in the mountains spellbound by the scenery. Over the next few days he travelled around the area visiting each and every famous spot, until seven days had passed. He felt a pang of homesickness and thought, "I had no idea how many days had passed. My mother and father are probably anxiously awaiting my return. So I shall bid this mountain farewell, and will rush home." So on August 25th he began his trek back to Kumage Castle.

The day of his departure Yujiro had visited various old ruins around Mt. Aso and thus it was nearly ten at night when he reached the spot just outside the city where the violent men had attacked him. The night was pitch dark since the sky was covered with layers of thick heavy clouds that completely blocked any light from the stars. Suddenly, from all sides there was the sound of bows being drawn. From the fields on either side of the road Yujiro heard the unmistakable sound of a multitude of arrows being fired in unison. The sky was thick with arrows and they fell like rain.

Yujiro understood in an instant what was happening,

"So, no doubt those evil bastards from the other day are still harboring a grudge, now they have set up another attack." Thinking fast, he came up with a plan, "I will make sure they use up all their arrows first!"

With that he dropped down to the ground and rolled on his side. He then took off his rain gear and drove the scabbard of his Katana into the ground, then hung his rain gear on it. Since it was pitch black outside, this served as a target for the archers' arrows which were still being shot in a great torrent, but they had no more effect than stalks of bamboo grass. Eventually, the intensity with which the various sorts of arrows were being shot slackened and stopped. The sound of thrumming bowstrings faded into the distance.

Yujiro rose up in a fury and knocked the scabbard holding his rain gear down and drew his sword. Just then the shapes of four or five men holding bows emerged from out of the tangled overgrown field. In addition, there were nearly a dozen men holding spears or Katana. In total fifteen or sixteen men began charging charging at Yujiro.

Among them were the same four thugs Yujiro had left half-alive and half-dead just a few days before, Kondo, Kumazawa and two others. The men had been stewing in their anger since the incident and had gotten together with other malicious compatriots. The group of sixteen men decided on a plan and began gatherings projectile weapons while others casually struck up conversations with Yujiro's acquaintances. Eventually they figured out his scheduled return date. Having determined when Yujiro would return home, the group waited to spring their violent trap.

奸人野外に矢を放つ圖
Illustration of Villains Shooting Arrows in a Field

奸人野外に矢を放つ圖
Illustration of Villains Shooting Arrows in a Field #2

Translator's Note: This is an illustration of the same scene from an 1851 version of this story titled *Miyamoto Musashi Legend of the Two Swords*. Judging by the severed head at the bottom of the illustration, this later edition increased the violence.

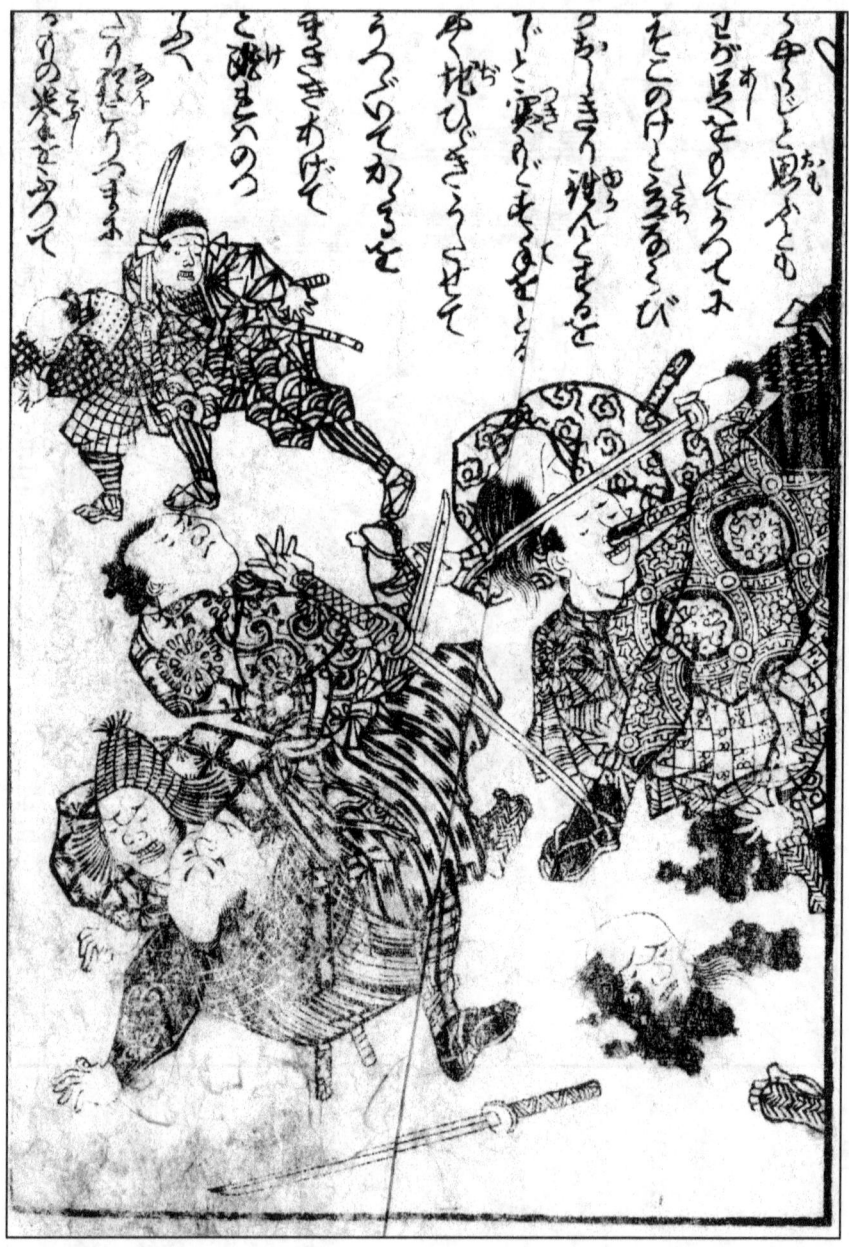

Translator's Note: From the 1851 *Miyamoto Musashi Legend of the Two Swords* 宮本無三四二刀傳
By Baitei Kinga 梅亭金鷲 & Utagawa Kunimaru 歌川国丸

As it turned out, despite the ambush, Yujiro's ability to react in a flash was nearly equal to that of a divine being. At the first sign of an ambush he employed the technique *Sloughing off the Cicada's Golden Shell*, which is from the *Thirty-Six Stratagems.* [5] He immediately dropped to the ground and rolled onto his stomach. Removing his rain gear, he propped it up so his attackers would mistake the shape for him and shoot at it. He used this strategy to exhaust his attackers' supply of arrows.

The villains fell for this trick hook, line and sinker. When Yujiro allowed his rain gear to fall over, the attackers were sure that it indicated Yujiro had been riddled with arrows. The men then took up their weapon and charged out from their hiding place, each hoping to be the first to strike the killing blow. However, Yujiro rose up to his full height and bellowed in a raging voice,

"You cowardly dogs! My attempt to resolve the situation amicably has been thrown back in my face. I see now that you need another demonstration of my ability. So, if that is what you desire, this time I promise each and every one of you will be cut."

With that declaration Yujiro drew his Katana and readied himself, to the eyes of the many villainous attackers it seemed as if he was rising up like a temple guardian god. So impressive was his stance that the attackers momentarily lost their momentum.

However, Yamauchi Kanimaru, on who's neck Yujiro had stomped during their previous encounter, harbored a furious rage and desire for revenge. He charged, fully committed, disregarding all thoughts of preserving his own life. Seeing Kanimaru's attack snapped the other villains out of their shock and they all cut or

---

5 *Thirty-Six Stratagems* 兵法三十六計 (Author unknown. Compiled circa 184 ~ 589 AD)
Chapter 4: Chaos Stratagems 混戰計
Sloughing off the Cicada's Golden Shell 金蟬脫殼 *Mask oneself. Either leave one's distinctive traits behind and become inconspicuous or masquerade as something or someone else. This strategy is mainly used to escape from a stronger enemy. This means leaving behind false appearances created for strategic purposes. Like the cicada shell, the facade remains intact, but the real action is now elsewhere.*

stabbed at Yujiro at the same time. Yujiro was now in the center of a group of 16 men swinging Katana and thrusting spears in swirls like Japanese clover blowing in the wind.

This time Yujiro moved with ten times their speed and, in his fury, his spirit made him take his long sword in his right hand and his short sword in his left. Swinging his two blades he was able to fend off the attacks of all sixteen men and not one of them was left uninjured.

From the outset Yujiro had no intention of killing the Samurai who were attacking him, though he easily could have. Since he was on a Shinobi no Tabi, or travelling incognito, he could not justify killing people. Thus, his primary concern was defending himself and escaping.

The battle began with the villains concealed in the undergrowth on all sides. Though they burst out simultaneously from concealed positions, none of them escaped uninjured. Yujiro swing his swords and cut them on across their head, cheek or nose. Several attackers took damage to their arms or elbows while Yujiro swept his sword across the legs of others. However, none of these cuts were a fatal blow.

Having finished, Yujiro sheathed his swords and strolled over to the side of the road, recovering his Kori, wicker travel trunk. Glaring at each injured man in turn declared with a look of disgust on his face, "I should go over and rip all your masks off, exposing your shameful faces but as I am not travelling in an official capacity I will leave you all here to rot. Next time you try something violent I will be unforgiving. If you do not have a change of heart, your household will lose all respect." And with that he resumed his journey home.

During his recent battle with the lunatics that attacked him, Yujiro had spontaneously developed and employed Nito, a two-sword style. Having created this method, he continued to develop and refine it and eventually the inner mysteries of the technique naturally became apparent to him. Yujiro's fame spread far and wide.

I would like to point out here that since the creation of Japan and the whole of the world there have been no other warriors who fought with two swords. Even in China there are no such warriors.

From time immemorial the only person to use Nito, two swords, is the founder of the Jutte "Ten Hands" School.[6]

Long ago, during the violent wars Kenbu Era (1334 ~ 1338) Nitta Yoshisada, a retainer of the Emperor, was engaged in the Battle of Minato River. This battle took place in July of 1336 in Settsu Domain, present day Hyogo Prefecture. Facing defeat, Nitta climbed up Motome Cliff and drew two swords, Devil Cutter and Devil Enclosing. Holding one in his right and the other in his left he cut and deflected the multitude of arrows being shot at him, until finally his horse collapsed beneath him, pinning his legs. Realizing he was trapped, Nitta cut his own head off.

Illustration of Nitta's final battle from: *Tale of Nitta Yoshisada's Life* 新田義貞一代記 1882. By Arakawa Kichigoro 荒川吉五郎

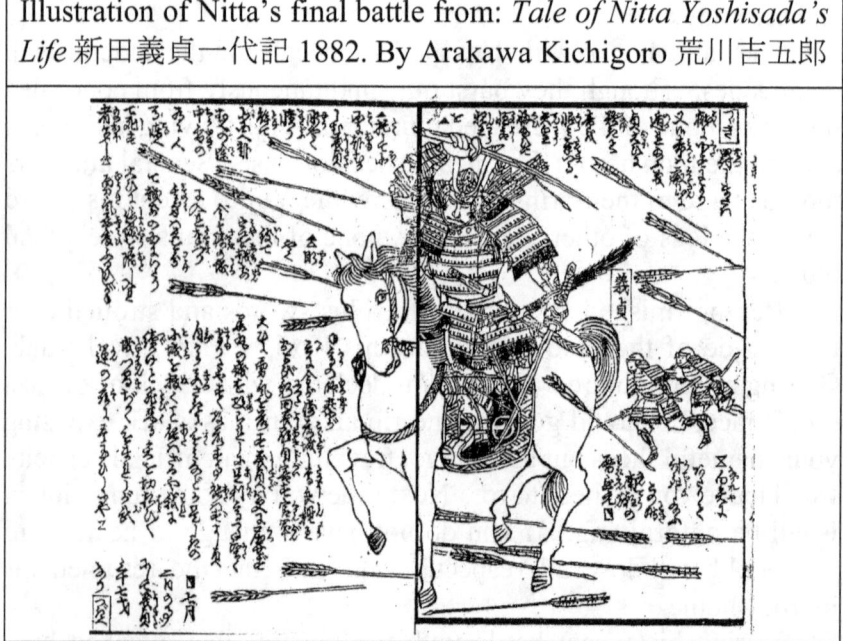

---

[6] The author implies Miyamoto Yujiro (Musashi) founded a school called *Jutte Ryu* or "The Ten Hands School," however Musashi's school is called Niten Ichi School. According to the Kokura Monument, which is the earliest record of Musashi's life, Musashi's father Shinmen Mujisai was a master of the Jutte, or truncheon, so the author may be referring to that. Also, a disciple of Miyamoto Musashi named Aoki Joemon founded a school called Tetsujin Jitte Ryu 鉄人実手流 however the Kanji are slightly different.

I would like to make clear that Musashi's Two-Sword School is still being taught today, much to his acclaim. Innumerable people have used his teachings to protect themselves.

So then, the rogue Samurai crawled out from every nook and cranny and looked over each other's injuries. Nearly all of them had cuts on their head or face while others were injured on the hands or legs. In other words, they all had Omote-Kizu, highly visible injuries. Realizing that later on these injuries would affect not only their appearance but their honor as well, they became depressed. The group did their best to bandage each other's wounds and, before dawn, they each returned home.

Later, even after their wounds had healed, the rogue Samurai found it difficult to return to their daily lives. They found themselves the target of rumors along the lines of, "So-and-so over there was part of a big group of Samurai that went after Yujiro, but they were humiliated." The group of 16 men had bungled the whole ambush and now they were seething with regret to the extent each was "gnawing at his own navel."

They lamented the fact that, if news of this incident reached the ear of Lord Kiyomasa, the consequences would be quite severe. Thus, after their wounds had completely healed the men left their posts at Kumage Castle and fled. No one knows where they went or what happened to them.

I would like to mention that there are numerous stories regarding the exploits of Miyamoto Musashi as a youth. Since the stories are convoluted and overlapping, recording all of them here would be impossible. Thus, I have included this episode and have abbreviated the rest.

宮本友次郎夢咄の圖
Illustration of Miyamoto Yujiro Dreaming

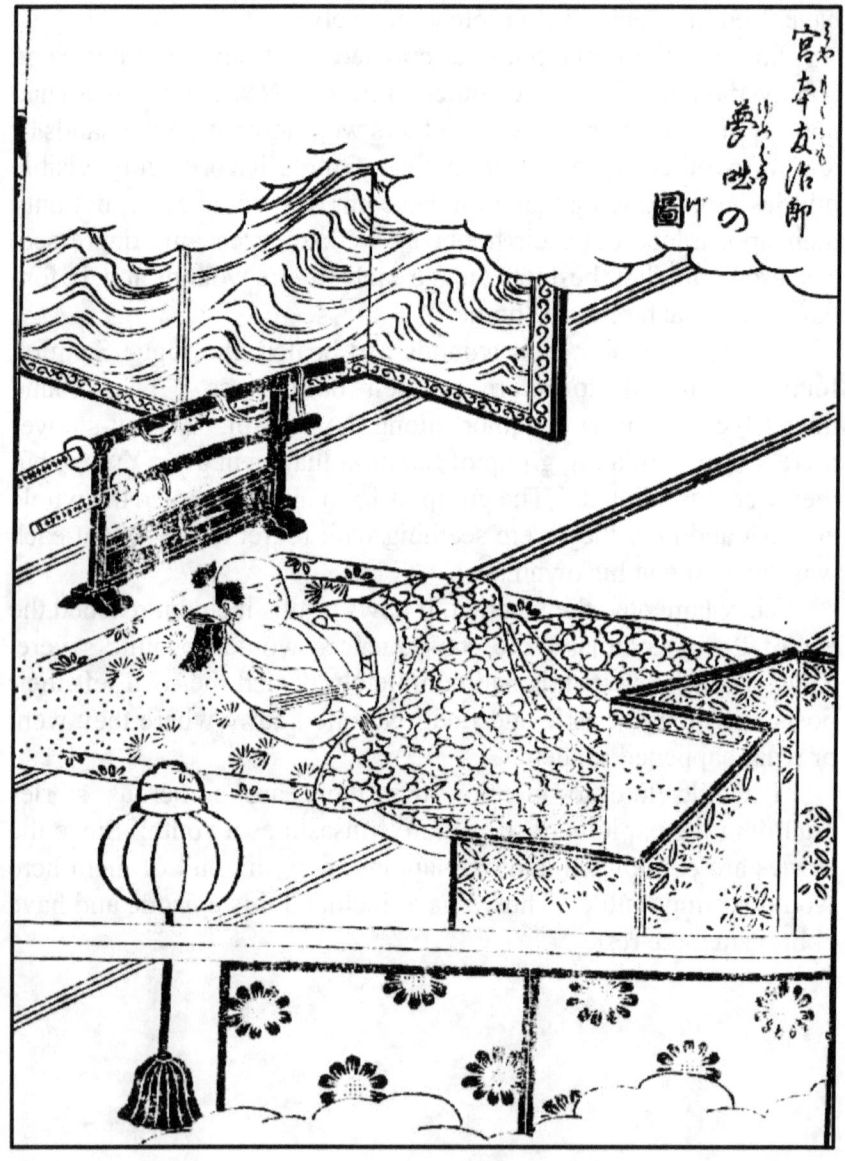

名島の高弟遺書於熊木事
A Letter Arrives at Kumage Castle From Yoshioka's Senior Students in Najima

The Chinese poet Liu Yong (987–1053) wrote,

A mother and father who raise a child without educating him or her means they have no love for their child.

A mother and father who raise and educate a child, only for him or her to refuse to learn means that child does not love him or herself.

Regarding the relationship between the Miyamoto father and son: From the day he adopted Yujiro, Buemon completely committed himself to educating him.　Yujiro, for his part, understood his duty and was diligent in his studies.　Miyamoto Yujiro made steady progress in the way of the sword and he developed into a proficient swordsman.　However, his progress did not stop there and within a few months he developed into a true expert.　By August of Tensho18 (1580) Yujiro had become enlightened to the inner mysteries of the sword and his skill surpassed that of his father.

On May 5th of that year many members of the Miyamoto Dojo gathered to pay their respects to the father and son for Tango-no-Sekku, the Boy's Day Celebration.　Miyamoto Buemon and his son poured Sake generously and paid their guests every courtesy.　As the party went on the topic turned to old war stories and even to Go-Oku, discussions evaluating the bravery or cowardliness of generals in recent battles.　They also discussed the skills of the Samurai serving the Miyamoto household.

In the midst of this conversation Yujiro interjected, "Recently I have been troubled by strange dreams that keep me from sleeping well at night.　Then, all the next day, I have an unsettled feeling. Just last week I dreamed of Yoshioka Taro Uemon, my birth-father in Najima.　I saw him mounted on top of enormous wild boar and he was riding up a mountain.　When I opened my eyes, I was shaking and even now I am having trouble relaxing.　I wonder if this portends some change in fortune, good or bad."

Some of the students prone to flattery said, "It surely means good things to come!"

宮本友次郎夢咄の圖
Illustration of Miyamoto Yujiro Dreaming #2

Others said something along the lines of, "It sounds to me like you may have a disease in one of your organs. Since my lord Yujiro trains in martial arts day and night, it is very likely your body and spirit are exhausted."

However, the thoughtful men furrowed their brows and didn't say anything. Suddenly, a young Samurai rushed up to the group and excitedly informed them, "A messenger from Najima has arrived."

The moment he heard this Yujiro's heart leaped into his throat. Upon further questioning it turned out that the letter that had arrived had been sent by Yoshioka's senior students.

He opened the letter and read.:

On the night of the 15th of last month your revered father was assassinated by persons unknown. He was on his way home from playing Go at Shinkanji temple. Your honorable mother, was so broken-hearted over the loss of Yoshida Taro Uemon that she succumbed to her illness and passed away.

Since Yoshioka Sensei was not from Najima he had no relatives here. Thus we, his students, arranged the funeral rites for the Yoshiokas. The Yoshioka line has now ended. We had intended to report this to you earlier, but with the sudden death of our teacher we temporarily forgot about everything else, however now we would like to make this report to you.

The rest of the letter contained further condolences.
Yujiro was thunderstruck and he could not even walk. His father, Buemon, was also reeling with an incomparable grief. The students of the Miyamoto school were all shaken to the core by the news and offered their profound sympathies to the father and son.

With tears in his eyes Buemon said, "I never imagined in all the wide world there was a Samurai more skilled with the sword than my great teacher. His faithful service to his lord was unsurpassed and he was ever humble about his skill with the Katana.

Though he was a well-known martial arts instructor, I cannot believe there was anyone who held a grudge against him. Also, despite the fact that he was assassinated in an ambush at night, the situation does not sound like the kind of attack that would have been carried out by one person. This attack was certainly done by expert sword instructors. I believe the assassins knew their skill with the sword could not compete with Yoshioka Sensei's, so they assassinated our teacher out of jealousy.

This means I have duty to take revenge for my teacher's assassination. Thus, I need to depart to Najima as soon as possible and speak directly to Yoshioka Sensei's senior students to see if they have any clues. While my intent is to avenge my teacher's death by confronting and killing his assassin, as a retainer of the Lord of Kumage Castle I cannot simply abandon my duties.

Yujiro, your birth-father has been murdered and you cannot allow his killer to remain alive under the same sky as the rest of the world, therefore you must depart immediately. In the meantime, it is necessary that I explain the details of this situation to our lord, and formulate a plan."

So they immediately drafted a reply letter and sent it off to Najima, then Buemon and his son wrote a Adauchi no Gansho, application for permission to embark on a revenge killing, and submitted it to Lord Kiyomasa.

絵本二島英勇記　卷三　終
End of Book 3

巌流敵討繪本二島英勇記
Revenge Killing of Ganryu: Two Islands (Swords)
An Illustrated Tale of Bravery
Volume IV

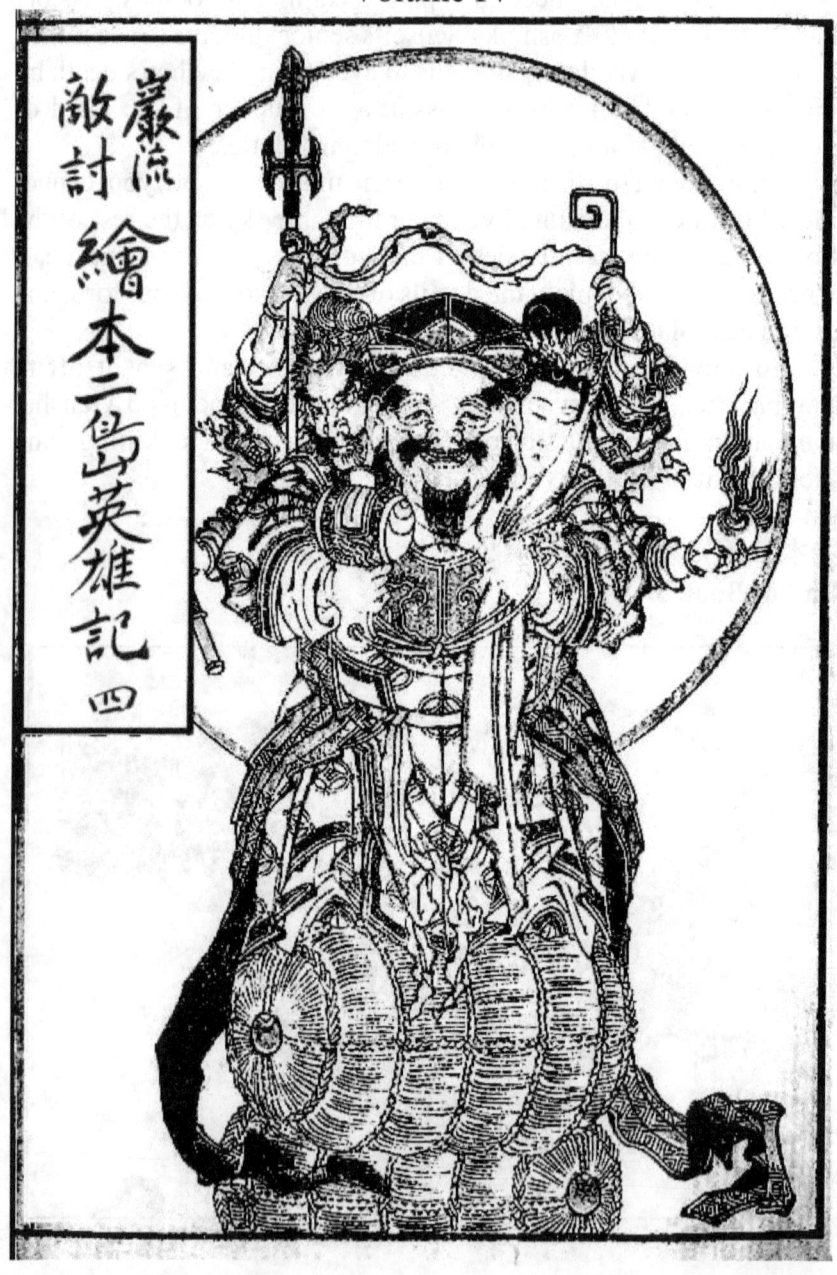

Book 4
Table of Contents

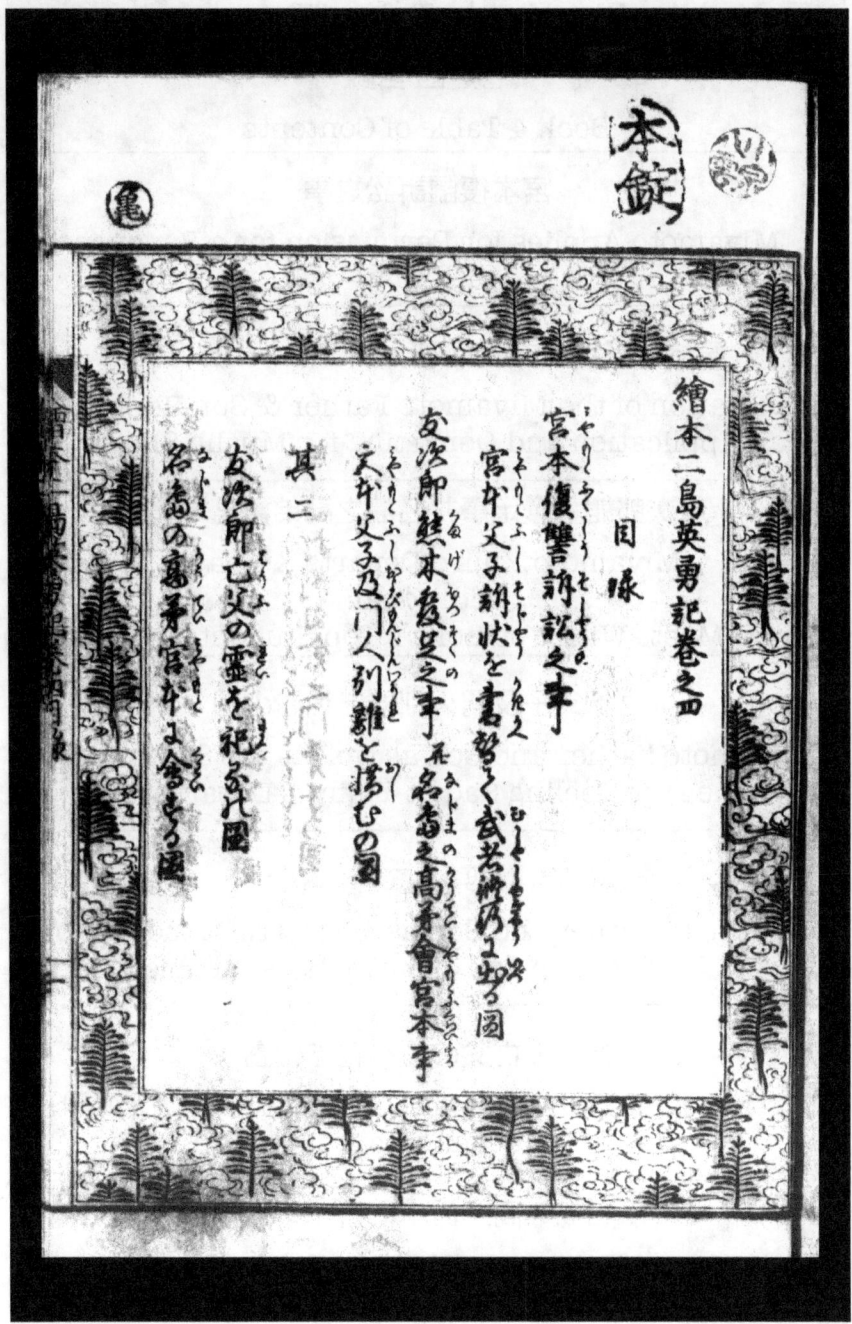

繪本二島英勇記
Two Swords
An Illustrated Tale of Bravery

巻之四 目録

Book 4 Table of Contents

宮本復讎訴訟之事

Miyamoto Applies for Permission for a Revenge Killing

宮本父子訴状を書替て　武者修行に出る圖

Illustration of the Miyamoto Father & Son Rewriting an Application and Departing for Musha Shugyo

友次郎熊木發足事并名島之高弟曾宮本事

Miyamoto Yujiro Departs Kumage
Additional:
Yujiro Meets With Yoshioka's Top Students in Najima

宮本父子及門人別離を惜むの圖

Miyamoto Father and Son as well as the Students of the Dojo Feeling Sad at Yujiro's Departure.

其　二

Miyamoto Father and Son as well as the Students of the Dojo Feeling Sad at Yujiro's Departure # 2

友次郎亡父の霊を祀るの圖

Illustration of Yujiro Paying His Respects at His Birth-Father's Grave

名島の高弟宮本に會する圖

Illustration of Miyamoto Meeting the Senior Students of Yoshioka's Dojo in Najima

Book 4
Table of Contents

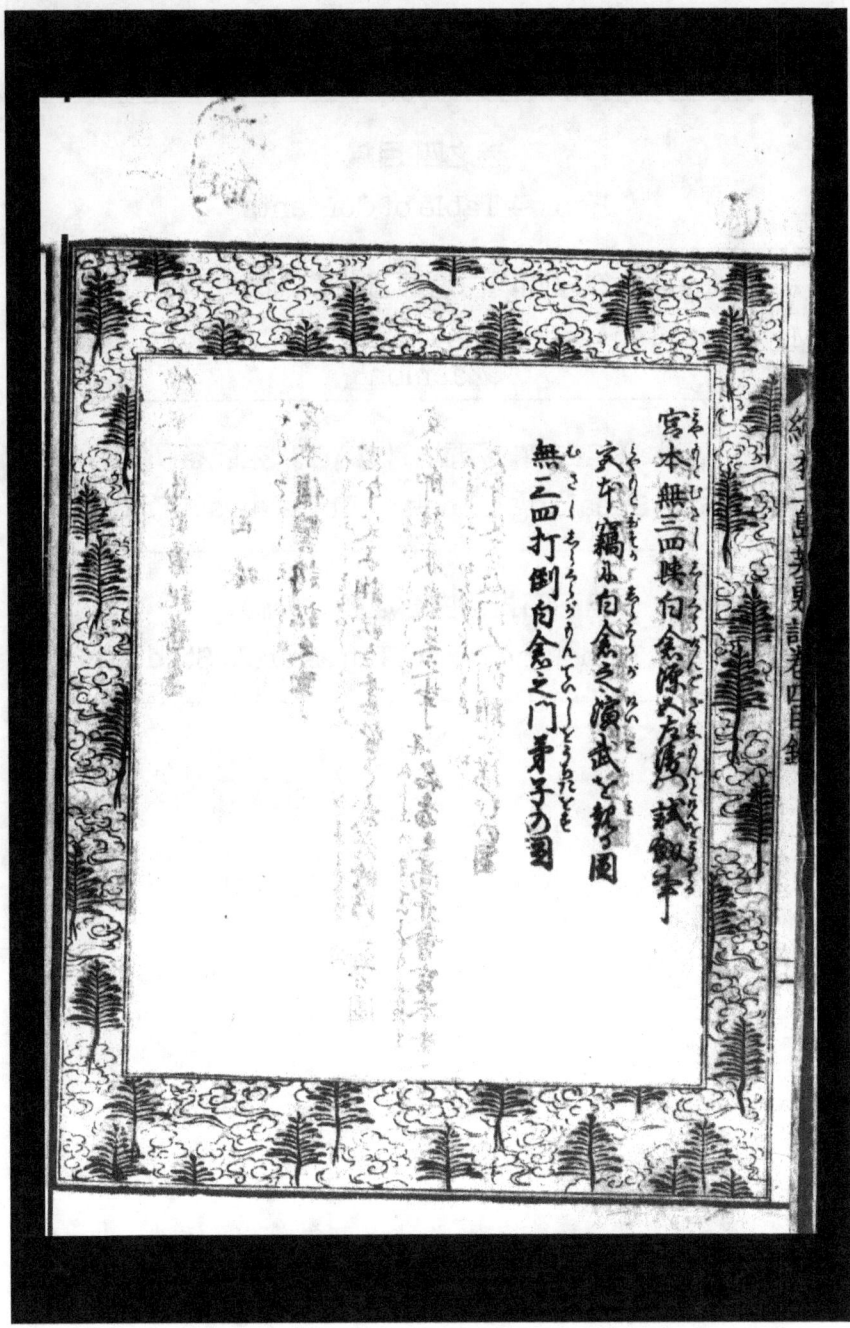

繪本二島英勇記
Two Swords
An Illustrated Tale of Bravery

宮本復讎訴訟之事
Miyamoto Applies for Permission for a Revenge Killing

子曰。善人爲邦百年、亦可以勝殘去殺矣誠哉是言也。
Master Confucius said: "If good men were to govern a country for a hundred years, they could overcome cruelty and do away with killing. How true this saying is!"[7]

- The Analects of Confucius 論語

Recently the Guardian of Rikuoku, Sassa Narimasa, who was in charge of Higo Domain, had failed to maintain order. There was a revolts all over his domain and many battles were being fought. Frustrated with Narimasa's incompetent reign, Lord Toyotomi Hideyoshi granted him the gift of death and installed Sato Kiyomasa, the head of the imperial accounting bureau, as lord of Kumage Castle. [8]

---

[7] From the section Zi Lu (542 ~ 480 BC.) This section is a series of questions posed by Zi Lu to Confucius. Translated by A. Charles Muller

[8] Sassa Narimasa 佐々成政 (1536 ~ 1588) was a real person and he was replaced by Kato Kiyomasa, whose name was changed from *Kato* Kiyomasa to *Sato* Kiyomasa for this story. He was given control of Higo Domain by Toyotomi Hideyoshi, however in 1588, due to difficulties in suppressing a series of local revolts, he was "given the gift of death" meaning he was ordered to commit suicide by Hideyoshi.

Hanagasaki Moriaki's 花ヶ前盛明編 book *Everything About Sassa Narimasa* 佐々成政のすべて discusses the event:

In February of 1588 Sassa Narimasa went to Osaka to apologize for failing to suppress the revolts in Higo Domain. Hideyoshi refused to meet with him and Sassa went into seclusion. Hideyoshi then replaced Sassa with Kato Kiyomasta as the head of Higo Domain and ordered Sassa to commit Seppuku for his failure.

The scene of Sassa's suicide was dramatic. He took the Tanto short knife and drew straight line across his abdomen, reaching in Sassa grabbed his own entrails and threw them at the ceiling.

Within three years of his appointment, Lord Sato Kiyomasa was able to stabilize the country and restore peace. He then embarked on various infrastructure projects including renovating Kumage Castle. All of these projects were now nearing completion.

Around this time Lord Hideyoshi was in Kyoto. Since May of Tensho 18 (1590) Hideyoshi had been engaged in a siege of Odawara Castle in Sochu Domain. It was being defended by Hojo Ujimasa and Hojo Ujinao and, despite the assault, the castle complex was proving resistant to the attackers' efforts[9].

When news of the siege reached Kumage Castle, Lord Kiyomasa assembled his senior advisors and asked for their advice on the possibility of setting out on horseback with his army for Soshu to assist with the siege. The advisors were unified in their response. "With our Domain back in order, all the construction projects finished and the castle renovated, would not travelling with our army to Odawara be appropriate?"

As the discussion continued, and everyone was giving their opinions Shobayashi Hayato [10] entered, kneeled before Lord Kiyomasa, bowed, and presented him a letter.

Hayato explained, "This is a document submitted by Miyamoto Buemon. In summary, since Yoshioka Taro Uemon was murdered

---

[9] Hojo Ujimasa 1538~1590 held out for three months from April to July of 1690. Completely surrounded both on land and sea, the Hojo situation became untenable. On July 1, 1690 the Hojo began negotiations with Toyotomi Hideyoshi and on July 5th an accord was reached. The lives of the defenders would be spared if Hojo Ujimasa committed Seppuku, which he did on July 11th 1690. He was 53 years old at his death.

Hojo Ujinao (1562~1591), Ujimasa's son, was not made to commit Seppuku since he was the son-in-law Tokugawa Ieyasu, however he and his wife were banished to the Mount Koya temple complex in Wakayama Prefecture. In February of 1591 he was pardoned by Hideyoshi who granted him a new fiefdom worth 10,000 Koku. He travelled to Osaka to begin his new role as a retainer of Hideyoshi but he died of smallpox in November of 1591.

[10] Shobayashi Hayato 隼人一心 (?~1631) was a real person. His name was Kazutada, however he was known as Hayato.

in unusual circumstances, Miyamoto Buemon's adopted son, Yujiro, would like permission for Kataki-uchi[11], to hunt down and kill the murderer. This is the substance of this application."

Kiyomasa scanned the document himself and was clearly startled by its content.

"Yoshioka is a well-known Samurai, and his name is famous in every corner of Japan. Even I have heard of him. Miyamoto Buemon was a member of Yoshioka's Dojo and was able to attain mastery of the inner secrets of the Yoshioka school of sword. In other words, Buemon's relationship to his sword instructor was as close as if Yoshioka was his father. Further, since Yoshioka is Yujiro's father by birth, there is no way he can ignore the situation. However, there is something I need to speak with these two about. Summon the father and son, Miyamoto Buemon and Miyamoto Yujiro.

Hayato immediately dispatched a messenger to the Miyamoto household, and the father and son quickly made their way to the castle. As soon as they arrived, Hayato brought the two before the lord of the castle. Buemon looked at the imposing Samurai in the room. In two rows sat Lord Kiyomasa's valiant warriors, Kato Mimasaka, Iida Kakubei, Akaboshi Taro Hyoei, Morimoto Gidafu and Saito Tatemoto[12]. The scene was very intimidating. Lord Kiyomasa spoke to the father and son from the far end of the room.

"I have carefully reviewed the document you submitted to me earlier. In summary, Yujiro, you wish permission to embark on an Adauchi, revenge killing, for the death of your birth-father Yoshioka. While this is an obvious request for you to make, I would like to step back and summarize the situation."

"Buemon, at the time you adopted Yujiro as your heir, Yoshioka still had another son. Unfortunately, the son passed away before his father, thus now there is no one to avenge Yoshioka's murder."

---

[11] This book uses the words Fukushu 復讐 "revenge" and Kataki-uch 敵討ち "killing your enemy" to describe revenge killing. Other words are Ada-uchi 仇討ち which also means "revenge killing."

[12] All the names are of real people who were retainers to Lord Kato Kiyomasa.

宮本父子訴状を書替て　武者修行に出る圖

Illustration of the Miyamoto Father & Son Rewriting an Application and Departing for Musha Shugyo

"Overall, the principle is sound, Buemon you have a master-apprentice relationship to Yoshioka and, you, Yujiro wish to avenge your birth-father's murder. Therefore, as father and son, you should set out, find the murderer and avenge Yoshioka's death. That being said, though I have searched my memory, in all of Japan, I have never heard of a man, adopted by another family, leaving them in order to extract vengeance for the death of his birth-father. The law is not for personal use, thus I cannot authorize Kataki-uchi, seeking out the murderer and killing him."

"In addition, Yoshioka is a Samurai serving the Kobayakawa household, while you, Miyamoto father and son, are part of my household. I believe it would be difficult to go by the name "Miyamoto" as you seek out the murderer, confront him and cut him down. It is going to be hard to explain why you are doing this revenge killing if you do not return to your original name, Yoshioka. Yujiro, taking such an action would be the same as casting aside the profound duty you have to honor your adoptive father who raised you since you were a baby. And Buemon, no doubt you would be more than a little uncomfortable about severing the relationship between you and your adopted son."

"Further, if Yujiro successfully discovers the whereabouts of the murderer, confronts him and succeeds in avenging Yoshioka's murder, logically Yujiro would then take your father's place in service to Lord Kobayakawa. The thought of losing a young retainer that has succeeded in such a task to another household is not something I, Kiyomasa, relish. However, taking all this into account I believe I may have struck upon an idea that will solve this, though I am hardly blessed with a great intellect."

"Yujiro, if you agree to the conditions I set out, you will be able achieve your goal of avenging your birth-father without having to sacrifice the respect and honor you hold for your adopted father. Both of these goals can be achieved. What do you think? Would you like to hear what I have to say about this or not?"

All the assembled Samurai felt that Kiyomasa was truly a thoughtful and brave man. One that never slandered others and was compassionate. Though these Samurai served him, he never abused their loyalty.

The Miyamoto father and son could feel sweat dripping down their backs as they listened to their lord, and felt immense relief and gratitude for his words. They pressed their heads down to the tatami mats and said, "Your consideration for our situation is completely unwarranted, No matter what you suggest we will not turn our backs to you. We are extremely grateful that you will consider our situation. We are prepared to accept any terms you offer."

Lord Kiyomasa began again, this time with a smile on his face. "Every story that I have ever heard regarding the murder of a great swordsman was invariably due to the fact they had incurred the wrath of another person. I imagine that it is the same in Yoshioka's case, he somehow incurred the anger of another person which led that person to decide to murder your teacher."

"If you examine his younger years or when Yoshioka was travelling the country doing Shugyo, intensive training, you will invariably find many swordfighters he defeated. Undoubtedly, the murderer is one of these men. Also, considering who Yoshioka was, anyone facing off against him would undoubtably have been a swordsman of remarkable skill and probably a senior instructor of some school."

"So, what I propose is that, you, Yujiro, will not embark on Kataki-uchi, but rather travel about as a man doing Musha Shugyo, or as a martial artist traveling around Japan seeking to develop his swordsmanship. By using "a journey of training" as a pretext you should first travel to Kyushu and seek out the well-known martial artists residing in the nine domains that make up that island. Then spend a few days or a fortnight in each area becoming familiar with the local martial artists. You can do this by discussing your training and your journey. I think that by doing this you will eventually you will start to pick up clues."

"While you are doing this, do not forget your purpose is to honor your family and find justice. If you do this, then as long as the sun still rises in east and the moon doesn't crash into the earth, you will absolutely achieve your goal. Do you have any doubt in this regard? While I cannot grant you permission for Kataki-uchi, I have no issue granting you permission to embark on Musha Shugyo, a pilgrimage to develop your sword art. I think as father and son you should consider my offer."

宮本父子及門人別離を惜むの圖
Miyamoto Father and Son as well as the Students of the Dojo Feeling Sad at Yujiro's Departure

宮本父子及門人別離を惜むの圖其二
Miyamoto Father and Son as well as the Students of the Dojo Feeling Sad at Yujiro's Departure #2

All of the Samurai in attendance were very impressed by Lord Kiyomasa's reasoning and decision. Neither Buemon nor Yujiro had the slightest issue with their lord's decision and they immediately accepted, rewrote the application and again presented it to their lord.

Straightaway Lord Kiyomasa invited Yujiro to sit by his side and offered him a shallow dish of Sake to celebrate his departure. With that, official permission was completed and they returned home.

友次郎熊木發足事并名島之高弟曾宮本事
Miyamoto Yujiro Departs Kumage
Additional:
Yujiro Meets With Yoshioka's Top Students in Najima

Miyamoto Yujiro returned home after receiving permission to embark on Musha Shugyo, a training pilgrimage, all over Japan. When he arrived Buemon was preparing items for Yujiro's journey. Buemon's wife was thrilled that Yujiro had received permission to depart. Over the long years Yujiro had lived in their household she had developed no small amount of affection for him.

She reflected, "Though he is planning to return from this journey, seeing him depart I am overcome with sadness. When will I see him again? The journey Yujiro set out on has no fixed destination, it's like trying to see the edges of a cloud on an overcast day. I wonder what will happen to him?" As she watched him leave, there were tears in her eyes.

Yujiro's younger brother Tomo-no-suke, who looked much older despite having turned 6 this year, was in tears over the departure of his older brother. In addition, all the members of the Miyamoto Dojo arrived one after the other to exchange low dishes of Sake as part of the departure ceremony. Having completed all his preparations and said his goodbyes, Yujiro set out at the Hour of the Sheep, or 2 pm, for his journey to avenge the murder of his birth-father.

It was a tradition from long in the past to depart on the day you receive leave from your lord, but Yujiro was also quite eager to get underway. The members of the Miyamoto Dojo accompanied

Yujiro for about 2 Ri, 8 kilometers, whereupon the escort stopped, lined all their horses up with their noses facing the direction Yujiro would travel, and performed various ceremonies before returning home.[13]

So then, Yujiro traveled to Najima at best possible speed. The first thing he did was to visit the grave of his birth-father Yoshioka Taro Uemon and pay his respects. Placing flowers on the grave and lighting incense, he brought his hands together in prayer and, overcome with grief, he prayed.

"If the spirit of my father is under me now, let him look into the very core of my being. I was separated from my mother and father when I was still a baby, and thus I was never, even once, able to honor you, my birth father, in the way that I should have. And now, someone has murdered you. In the end I was not able even to conduct a funeral for my own mother and father. Because of this my heart and lungs are fit to burst apart with sadness."

"However, even if the murderer hides in one of the nine layers of heaven or nine levels below the earth I will search him out. Then I will cut his body into ten-thousand pieces one thousand times over in order to assuage the grief and anger I feel for my father's passing."

His eyes glared fiercely as he ground his teeth, not noticing the tears that fell like rain. Next Yujiro went to his mother's grave. It feels like even now she is pestering me as if she were alive. Later, he visited the houses of Yoshioka's senior students and thanked each of them personally.

Having done this, he returned to the inn where he was staying. It wasn't too long before Yoshioka's students began to gather at the inn.

They said to Yujiro, "Following the strange death of your father we traveled to every corner of this domain searching for clues, but, so far we have not found anyone who held a grudge against Yoshioka Sensei."

---

[13] The *Uma no Hana-muke* 餞, "Direction of the horse's nose" ceremony. This ceremony done some distance from the traveler's starting point. Those accompanying the traveler point the noses of their horses in the direction of travel in addition to exchanging gifts, reciting poetry and drinking cups of Sake.

友次郎亡父の霊を祀るの圖
Yujiro Paying His Respects at His Birth-Father's Grave

"Yoshioka, who was our Sensei and father, was humble man who never put on airs. He never slandered or insulted the heads of other schools or their instructors. He was respectful to all the Samurai he met, moreover, we have never heard of him starting an argument with anyone. In the whole of Kyushu island there is no one that knew him, or even who didn't know him, that is not distraught by his senseless murder. However, it seems unlikely that anyone other than a man filled with hatred could have been able to cut down a peerless warrior like our father and teacher Yoshioka Sensei."

The students continued, "As we considered the circumstances, we recalled that in early august Yoshioka Sensei applied for leave to visit the Onsen in the Arima area of Sesshu Domain. He happened to stop by the town under Himeji Castle in Sesshu Domain on his way home. Though he only stayed one night there, something unexpected happened. Yoshioka Sensei and a man named Sasaki Ganryu got into an argument. We also heard that apparently, Ganryu was adamant that our teacher gravely insulted him. It seems likely that bastard Sasaki Ganryu is the one responsible."

"After concluding Ganryu was the likely suspect, we again reviewed the circumstances surrounding the murder of our teacher and father. Clearly, he was killed with one powerful cut from behind. The blow entered the top of his right shoulder and extended all the way down to the ribs on his left side. Judging by this cut, we determined the person handing the sword was a highly-skilled Samurai. The only other cut on the body was the Todome, or coup de grâce, in the throat."

"It was at this point that Samurai in the nearby Nario household heard the sound of a sword cutting. Startled, they raced outside and they reported hearing the sounds of retreating footsteps from both the east and west. Thus, though rumors abound, we can only conclude that the attack was the work of more than one assailant.

"To determine the whereabouts of Ganryu we dispatched a man to Himeji. Within 5 or 6 days a Hikyaku, running messenger, should be here with a report. Once we have that report, you can make your departure."

The efforts Yoshioka's senior students had made greatly relieved Yujiro and expressed his gratitude to the senior students of Yoshioka,"I am deeply moved by the dedication of you, the senior students of my birth-father. Let us wait for the messenger to arrive and then decide what to do. Thanks to your astute observations it seems beyond a doubt that Ganryu was responsible." The senior students then all departed.

After 6 or 7 days the senior students returned and reported. "Today the Hikyaku running messenger we sent to Sesshu returned. He was able to observe the area and make inquiries. Last year, after Ganryu and Yoshioka suddenly clashed, the incident resulted in Ganryu completely losing face in front of his students. Right after, he virtually fled the Himeji area and no one knows where he went. There is no doubt that Ganryu was the one who did it."

Yujiro was delighted and said, "All your efforts have been worthwhile. Now I know the person to extract my revenge on. At first everything was extremely vague, but now that I have heard this report, I can focus on my target. So then, in all likelihood, Ganryu, the man that murdered my father, changed his name. However, since I don't know what Ganryu looks like I will need to speak to the servant that accompanied my father Taro Uemon to the Onsen inn Arima. He can surely describe Ganryu's appearance. Where is he now?"

Yoshioka's students responded, "Yes, about him… Last winter he took leave to return to his home, but he got sick and died suddenly. He actually passed away before our teacher and father did."

Yujiro replied, "That is extremely unfortunate. However, from days of old, avenging the murder of your father or lord was never an easy task. I will trust that the heavens above will be watching as I seek to complete my task."

Yujiro then set about again readying his things for departure. He went around to the houses of all the senior students and offered his thanks. Then, choosing an auspicious day, he left Najima. He decided then to change his name to Miyamoto Musashi 宮本無三四, using three Kanji that mean, "No-Three-Four."[14]

---

[14] Musashi's name is written 武蔵 "martial-storehouse." Miyamoto Musashi's father was named Mujisai 無二斎 which contains the word "no-two" so "no-three-four" could be related to that.

名島の高弟宮本に會する圖

Illustration of Miyamoto Meeting the Senior Students of Yoshioka's Dojo in Najima

宮本無三四、白倉源五左衛門と剣を試合う事
Miyamoto Musashi & his Duel with Shirakura Gengo Zaemon

At this time, Lord Toyotomi Hideyoshi had assumed complete control of every domain, and one could say that all the lands surrounded by the four seas had fallen into his hand. However, *it was not yet time to release the oxen into the fields around Peach Grove.*[15] Thus, in every domain in Japan the noisy sounds of men conducting intense martial arts training reverberate morning and night. The current lord of Okayama Castle in Bizen Domain was state minister Ukita Hideie.[16] Every Samurai under his command learned a martial art and the sounds of martial training emanated from every Dojo unceasingly, day and night.

---

[15] This Chinese expression is from the <u>Successful Completion of the War</u> chapter of the *Book of Documents* by an unknown author in the 5th century BC.

Book of Documents 書經 : <u>Successful Completion of War</u>
武成惟一月壬辰 旁死魄。越翼日 癸巳 王朝步自周，于征伐商

In the first month, the day Ren-chen immediately followed the end of the moon's waning. The next day was Gui-ji, when the king, in the morning, marched from Zhou to attack and punish Shang.
厥四月，哉生明，王來自商，至于豐。乃偃武修文，歸馬于華山之陽，放牛于桃林之野，示天下弗服

In the fourth month, at the first appearance of the moon, the king came from Shang to Feng, when he hushed all the movements of war, and proceeded to cultivate the arts of peace. He sent back his horses to the south of mount Hua, and let loose his oxen in the open country of Tao-lin, showing to all under heaven that he would not use them (again).
Translated by James Legge 1815 ~ 1897

[16] Ukita Hideie 宇喜多秀家 (1573~1655) was a real person, though this book writes his name with two Kanji 浮田 instead of three Kanji 宇喜多, though the names are read the same. Ukita fought against Tokugawa Ieyasu in the Battle of Sekigahara in 1600, and was exiled to Hachijo Island, where he died.

Amongst the various teachers of martial arts in this domain was a man named Shirakura Gengo Zaemon. While he was staying at Kibitsu Shrine 吉備津神社 when he received a divine dream which inspired him to create his own school, which he called Kibi Shindo Ryu. He had become the dominant sword instructor in Bizen Domain and his name reverberated beyond the borders of Bizen into neighboring domains. Lord Hideie, having heard about this teacher, rashly gave the man his trust despite the fact that Shirakura was arrogant and seemed to view other people as something less than bugs. Seeing his attitude, the Samurai who served Lord Hideie found Shirakura contemptable.

On September 17th of Tensho 19 (1591) Shirakura called all his students together. He then divided them into two groups, and called one East and the other West. He then had one student from East fight a duel with a student from West. The winner stayed in his group and fought round after round. If a student succeeded in knocking down three opponents he would receive prize money, a present or Shirakura would send words of praise to Lord Hideie. Shirakura held such contests six times a month. Other times there would be Wa-ke Jiai, duels amongst smaller groups within Shirakura's Dojo.

Today a Wa-ke Jiai competition was being held at the Dojo, so many students had arrived early in the morning and the sounds of wooden swords crashing together could be heard from outside the Dojo. If you pricked up your ears even a person traveling down the main road could hear it.

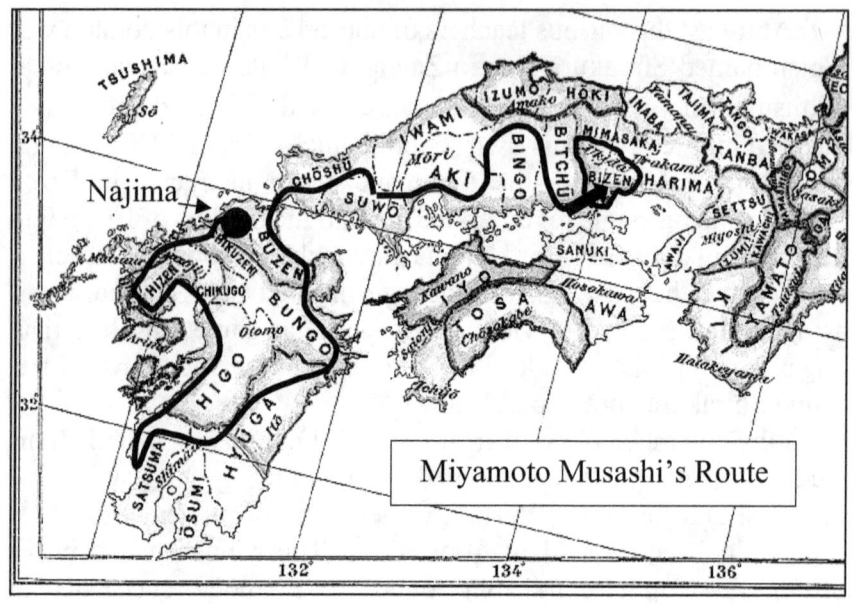

Miyamoto Musashi's Route

At around this time Miyamoto Musashi[17] had left Najima and travelled through each of the nine domains in Kyushu. Having completed this circuit, he traveled up through the Chugoku region. It goes without saying he passed through Suwō and Choshu, before traversing Aki Domain and Bingo Domain to get to Bichu Domain.

Along the way he dueled with the renowned (martial) artists in each area, but not one of them could offer Musashi a challenge. Seeing that clearly none of the Samurai he faced were skilled enough to be the object of his revenge he mused, "I need to head towards the upper regions of Japan, Kyoto and Osaka…"

As he passed through the town below Okayama Castle in Bizen Domain, he was amazed at how vibrant the area was. The city was bustling in a way he had never seen in other domains and Musashi felt he was unable to find the words to describe it. There were Samurai with bows and arrows on their shoulders leading horses with determined looks on their faces. Musashi found himself wandering around aimlessly. Then, quite unexpectedly, he ended up in front of Shirakura Gengo Zaemon's residence.

---

[17] From now on the story refers to him as Miyamoto Musashi.

There was a gate in the front of the wall and the Dojo, a long rectangular building, was on the other side of the wall. From inside the shouts of young warriors could be heard out on the street. Musashi stopped outside the gate and thought, "It sounds like there is a training hall for Samurai on the other side of this wall. I wonder who the teacher is and what school he teaches? I would very much like to see some of their training. I, Musashi, have never heard of the Shirakura Dojo before…"

As he stood there trying to catch a glimpse of the training, he noticed the house seemed to be that of a Samurai of average rank, who did not even warrant a guard at the gate. Musashi mused to himself, "This is lucky, I can catch a diagonal glimpse of the training they are doing in the Dojo through this little section of broken wall…"

Just then a young Samurai happened to step out of the compound. He immediately noticed Musashi and shouted in a loud, angry voice, "Just who the hell are you?! Sneaking around the house and trying to steal glimpses of our training! On top of that you destroyed part of the wall…what an unbelievably outrageous act!"

He continued, "And looking at the way you are dressed, the few belongings you have on your back and your unfamiliar face… I surmise you are from another domain. So now I am even more suspicious!"

In face of this severe berating, Musashi took off his Anri, woven bamboo grass travel-case, and tried to apologize and explain in a courteous manner, "I am a traveler and am wholly unfamiliar with the geography of this area. I happened to be passing through this area with many residences and lost my way. Quite by accident I ended up in front of this house and heard voices raised in martial training. Thinking *Well, well, well, This is a fine sound!* and before I knew it I had stepped in the mud at the base of the wall and peered in at your training. I humbly ask your forgiveness for this transgression. Chipping out a hole in your wall in order to spy on your training would truly be a dire offense however, I must ask you to pardon me on this offence as the hole I was peering through was already there." The man showed no inclination to accept Musashi's explanation and said gruffly,

"You come with me!" and he grabbed Musashi's arm and pulled him.

宮本竊に白倉之演武〔けいこ〕を観る圖
Miyamoto Sneaking a Look at Shirakura's Training

Translator's Note: The same scene but from an undated version:
True Record of Miyamoto Musashi 宮本無三四実伝記
By Gakutei Teikou 岳亭 定岡 1786～1868
Illustrated by Ikkousai Yoshimori 一光斎 芳盛

Musashi was peering at Shirakura's training when members of the Dojo discovered him and challenged him to a duel.

Translator's Note: The same scene from the 1851 *Miyamoto Musashi Legend of the Two Swords* 宮本無三四二刀傳 By Baitei Kinga 梅亭金鷲 & Utagawa Kunimaru 歌川国丸

Note: This illustration shows the Dojo members with their training gear, including facemasks tied onto their Shinai training swords and carried on their shoulder.

Hearing the commotion outside the Dojo, numerous young Samurai came running out shouting, "I don't care what's going on, let's make it bigger!" Overlapping voices shouted, "What is happening?! Where is it happening?!"

The man who seized Musashi said, "He is making all kinds of excuses!" All the young Samurai shouted their conclusion, "He is a scoundrel! It doesn't matter what he has to say, the whole country is at war! He is likely a Kanja or Saisaku or other such spy! Anyone who tries to sneak into our compound without a guide or permission can only be a thief attempting to steal. Its best to just cut him apart without any fuss!"

And with that they all began running to grab their swords. Just then, from inside the Dojo, a loud voice rang out. "You men cease this barnyard shouting!" The young men sheathed their swords and parted so a man about 40 years old could walk out between them.

Musashi looked up at the man and saw he was over 6 Shaku, 180 centimeters, with a round face, large eyes and a mustache hanging down from his cheeks and jaw. His arms were also thick with hair and he had not shaved to top of his head, but had it all pulled back and tied at the back of his head. He did not appear to be an ordinary man. All the other Samurai fell silent.

The man faced Musashi and said, "I am the person serving as the instructor at this Dojo. My name is Shirakura Gengo Zaemon. My lord traveler[18], I would like to know what domain you are from. Are you on a personal trip or are you on official business at the order of your lord? Please explain yourself."

Musashi answered in a way that showed he was not the least bit intimidated, "I am not serving as an official representative. I have been travelling to various domains doing Musha Shugyo. I will refrain from using my name for now. I have travelled from Kyushu and across the central Chugoku region and arrived here. Lord Shirakura, your name is well-known in martial arts circles. My first objective when I arrived in this domain was to seek you out and join your school as a student."

---

[18] The people all refer to each other as "lord" however this is showing deference among martial artists. The only real lord is the lord of the domain.

"I was hoping you would be willing to point out any deficiencies in my swordsmanship. Further, I wanted to see for myself the martial spirt and technique of the Samurai serving Lord Ukita. My intention was to locate your Dojo and visit tomorrow, however I, quite by chance, happened to end up in front of your residence. Having this unexpected chance to meet with you is quite fortuitous and I think it means good things will come of it. My humble request is that you allow me to join the training along with your other students. I would like to state that I do have Inka, an official scroll of rank, from a certain school of sword.[19]"

"If I find that my martial skills are inferior to yours, I would request that you serve as my teacher. Though I am an amateur with the sword, if you defeat me I will bend my waist till it breaks and sink to my knees to request you become my teacher, though it may cost you many days and months of effort. My request is that you engage me in a duel, and if you accept I would be delighted beyond words."

Shirakura Gengo Zaemon was a shrewd man who was not above deception. Earlier, when he told the young Samurai to stand down, his action was not born out of concern or compassion. In this era, with uncertain conditions prevailing all over the country, each domain was sending out Kansha, spies. Seeing the intense look in Musashi's eyes coupled with his traveler's attire lead Shirakura to conclude, "This man is likely a spy from a domain we are in conflict with. I will make him drop his guard and find out his true intentions. If he is a Kansha then I can lock him up until a ransom is paid, and if not, we can have fun cutting him to pieces."

The true reason Shirakura calmed down the Samurai was to use it as an excuse to question the traveler closely, however Musashi's answer surprised him. The master and his students all exchanged a look showing that the situation was different than they expected.

Shirakura was a daring man of incomparable talent. In addition, no man seemed to be his equal not only in Bigo Domain, but the surrounding domains as well.

---

[19] This means Musashi has trained extensively and received official recognition of his rank.

無三四打倒白倉之門弟の圖
Musashi Knocking Down Shirakura's Students

Seeing that Musashi was still very young, Shirakura seethed with rage inside thinking, "Shit…this baby in diapers. A calf born this year doesn't know anything about the fierceness of a tiger. I will knock him down with my wooden sword then break his hands and feet. I think I will quite enjoy watching him lying on the ground suffering half-alive and half-dead."

Showing none of his anger outwardly Shirakura said amicably, "Well then, you certainly do appear to be a man on Musha Shugyo. Please forgive my students hasty actions, they were not aware you were on the path of training. Truthfully, I should be the first to spar with you, however my lord ordered me to serve as the sword instructor for the whole of this domain. If my lord were to hear that I was your first opponent, he would be most displeased. Please duel with my senior students first. If you are not able to achieve victory over them, then it will no doubt serve as good training. So then, please give me your name and where you are from."

Musashi, hearing this, replied in an extremely gentle tone, "If, by some stroke of luck, I am able to achieve victory, I will not remain but immediately depart. If I am defeated, I will stay here you will be my teacher and I will be your student. If you are my teacher it is akin to being my father. In such a case I will be happy to tell you my name and where I am from. But that will happen at the end of the duels, when victory or defeat has been determined."

"With regards to dueling with your students first, I have no argument against that. I would like to mention that my school is Nito, meaning I use two swords. My opponent is welcome to use Shinken, a real sword, however, I will be satisfied to use these Bokuto, wooden swords. So then, honored students, please decide in which order you will duel."

Though there was no outward reaction from the senior students in Shirakura's Dojo, they all had an uneasy feeling inside. They waited for the sword master to indicate who should duel first.

Gengo Zaemon looked down the rows of his students and commanded, "Lord Fukuda Jusaemon, come to the center!" Immediately Jusaemon stood and tucked the sides of his Hakama into his belt high enough so that his thighs were showing. He brought his Bokuto up into Sha, or a diagonal stance, and leapt into the center of the training area. Musashi bowed once to the members of the Dojo who were seated and said, "Though I am travelling I am accustomed to using my own Bokuto. They are in my travel Anri case. I will fetch them and welcome you as my opponent."

He then quickly stood and pulled a dyed leather hakama printed with crests that looked like the Sho, a reed flute.[20] Having dressed he picked up a wooden sword in each hand and faced his opponent.

Shirakura and his students watched intently, not even blinking. Both combatants shouted and then began slowly closing the distance between them. Fukuda, determined to take Sen, the initial strike, brought his sword down in a straight line, aiming for the top of Musashi's head. Musashi raised his left sword to block this, then he leapt in and struck with his right sword so fast the action could hardly be seen. It was faster than when a spark flies off stone when struck with a sword. Fukuda Jusaemon was hit on the crown of his skull, right above his metal forehead plate and, still holding his Bokuto he crumpled down onto his butt. Though he was clearly dazed by the blow, he endured the pain, stood and shuffled to the side.

The instructor and every one of his students gasped in shock. Gengo Zaemon was thrown into a panic, and called out to another student, "Lord Murayama Genuemon, come out here!"

Murayama, called forward while he was in shock, turned his unease into anger and shouted, "I don't care who this man is from or where he is from! It doesn't matter if he is a devil[21] with three heads and six long arms, I will completely pulverize him!"

With that he leaped into the open space surrounded by Shirakura's students and faster than you can shout, "So then, prepare to surrender!" He thrust straight at Musashi's Miken, the spot between his eyebrows. Musashi responded as before, using the sword in his left hand to sweep this attack away. Then, employing the exact same technique as before, he struck with the sword in his right hand. Having been hit on the top of his head Murayama Genuemon withdrew.

---

[20] The Shō 笙 is a Japanese reed instrument
[21] The Samurai calls Musashi a *Tenma* "Heavenly Devil" which is a Buddhist creature that resides in the sixth heaven in the realm of desire who tries to prevent people from doing good

Translator's Note: The same scene from the 1851 *Miyamoto Musashi Legend of the Two Swords* 宮本無三四二刀傳.

By Baitei Kinga 梅亭金鵞
& Utagawa Kunimaru 歌川国丸

Having seen both Fukuda and Murayama defeated in the same way, the other students went pale. There was not a man amongst them who was not thinking, "Confronting a person of unknown origin and abilities resulted in this disaster, what a deplorable situation."

Shirakura's heart was thumping in his chest as he felt his panic rising, as he sent one high level student after another to duel. Takada Sennosuke, Fukushima Kinzaemon, Moriwaki Sajuro, Ukita Genbei, Inoko Takumi and Kaizawa Manuemon were all called out one after another. Eighteen men stepped out and all those who dueled with Musashi were struck. Then the next man who replaced him was hit and every one of them were knocked senseless. Musashi defeated all of them without using any tricks or clever schemes.

Shirakura shouted, "I have met many people over the years who have done training in Kenjutsu, the art of the sword, however never in all my life have I met a man of such a rare talent. Clearly your skills are beyond those of an average man. Thus, it seems time for you to face me. However, you have been attacked by one student after another for some time, perhaps you are tired and would like a break? First of all, why don't you have some tea and rest for a spell. After the break you and I can duel."

Musashi answered, "My art is still completely undeveloped. My victories here were only the result of temporary good fortune. I accept your order and I will take a break. Then I hope to be granted the chance to see the sword-work of the great Shirakura Sensei.

絵本二島英勇記　巻四　終
End of Book 4